TABOR EVANS

LONGARM
AND BIG TROUBLE IN BODIE

JOVE BOOKS, NEW YORK

LONGARM AND BIG TROUBLE IN BODIE

A Jove Book / published by arrangement with
the author

PRINTING HISTORY
Jove edition / September 1995

ISBN: 0-515-11702-1

A JOVE BOOK®
Jove Books are published by The Berkley Publishing Group,
200 Madison Avenue, New York, New York 10016.
JOVE and the "J" design are trademarks
belonging to Jove Publications, Inc.

PRINTED IN THE UNITED STATES OF AMERICA

10 9 8 7 6 5 4 3 2 1

Chapter 1

They say you were wild and woolly, Bodie,
And fast on the draw as they make 'em;
That you lived at ease with the bad and the bold,
Who thought nothing of shooting a man down cold,
And defying the law to take 'em.

—LILLIAN NINNIS

Longarm stood at the bar nursing a beer on an airless July afternoon as he awaited the arrival of the eastbound Union Pacific which would carry him back to Denver. He couldn't get out of town fast enough because Reno was sweltering in the heat of summer.

"It's too damned hot for anyone to go work less'n they gotta," the huge bartender named Fergus remarked, pouring himself a warm beer and tossing it down his gullet before drawing himself yet another.

"Well," Longarm said, removing his Ingersoll pocket watch from his vest and checking the time. "I've got to wait about another thirty minutes and then I can finally board the eastbound Union Pacific."

"Where you goin', Marshal?" the bartender demanded to know as he leaned his big arms on the bar.

"Back to Denver," Longarm said. "I've been away from my own bed for almost six months, and when I get home I'm going to sleep for about a week."

"Gonna be hot in Denver too," Fergus warned smugly, wiping the back of his running nose with his sleeve. "Train passenger from there came in just about two days ago and said it was over a hundred in Cheyenne. It's probably just as bad in Denver. Hotter than a whore's underwear."

When Longarm didn't say anything, the bartender continued. "If'n I was you, or if'n I could ever get away from this saloon and have a little time off, I'd head right on up the mountain and take my comfort in Lake Tahoe. That lake water is colder than a whore's heart."

"Sure," Longarm said, "I been up there lots of times, but I'm not on vacation."

"Meaning," Fergus said, cocking his eyebrow and looking at Longarm as if he were on trial, "that you are being paid this very minute to sit here and drink beer—by us poor taxpayers?"

Maybe it was the heat, the green beer, or the damned flies, but Longarm was feeling unusually testy. The bartender, a coarse man who could not shut up and mind his own business, was starting to become a real irritant.

"Taxpayers, hell," Longarm growled. "Fergus, I'll bet you never paid a tax in your whole life. And yeah, I'm on a salary. If they paid me by the hour, the government and its taxpayers would go practically broke."

"You're just saying that because you caught a couple of train robbers that was stealing the government mail," the bartender said, folding his big, hairy arms across his chest and jutting out his jaw. "From what I hear, you

2

were luckier than a whore on—"

"Shut up about the whores!" Longarm snapped, rocking back on his heels and balling his fists. Fergus was brutish-looking with a fist-busted nose, which Longarm was about to mash again. "Fergus, I came in here for a beer and some peace and quiet. But what do I get? A big-mouthed, ugly bastard who can't shut up and leave me alone."

Fergus's lantern jaw sagged and his own fists knotted. "You callin' me big-mouthed and ugly?"

"And you can add stupid too," Longarm said, easing back from the bar.

The bartender's face turned as red as raw meat. "I always hated lawmen, and you ain't doin' a damn thing to change that opinion."

"Maybe," Longarm said, feeling his blood start to rise, "you think that I care who you like or don't like."

"That ties it!" Fergus bellowed. "Get out of here before I throw you out!"

Longarm didn't move. "I'm going to finish my beer and leave when I want," he said, "unless you're even more stupid than you look and attempt to throw me out the door."

"Well, if you're man enough to keep that tin badge in your pocket, I will!" Fergus thundered.

"Then come on," Longarm said, deciding that the bartender's brain had probably become pickled from drinking too much of his own green beer.

Fergus charged around the bar and the handful of other patrons retreated toward the doorway. But Custis held his ground and when the bartender lunged at him, he flipped the last of his bad beer into Fergus's face and then ducked a wild overhand that stirred the hot air and scattered the droning flies.

3

Longarm was a big man himself, although now he was outweighed by at least fifty pounds. As he ducked, he drove his fist into the bartender's flabby gut. Fergus grunted and his mouth flew open. Greenish froth sprayed from his lips and his fist struck the bar, and he tried to hold himself up as Longarm pounded him twice in the kidney.

"Enough!" the bartender cried, knees buckling as he sagged toward the floor, puking in a cuspidor.

Longarm stepped back and eyed the man. "I never saw such an unsociable bartender in my life," he said, deciding that this fight was over and he might as well start off for the train depot and suffer the heat for a few extra minutes.

Longarm headed outside, where the air scorched him like the heat of a blacksmith's forge. Tugging the brim of his black Stetson down against the hot glare of the afternoon sun, he marched up Virginia Street.

"Marshal!"

Longarm heard the venom in Fergus's ragged voice, and knew before he went for his gun that the bartender was going to try and kill him. Even as Longarm's hand slapped the butt of his Colt, he threw himself sideways into Mrs. Baylor's Millinery Shop. Three shots boomed and Mrs. Baylor and her female clients dove for cover, screaming.

Longarm rolled into a crouch with his gun in his hand. He could hear Fergus's huge clodhoppers slamming down on the boardwalk as the man raced forward, intent on finishing Longarm off.

"Easy, ladies," Longarm warned. "Just stay low and remain calm!"

But there was nothing calm about them. They were all screaming as if their throats were being cut. Longarm

4

knew that he could not risk one of these hysterical women getting killed accidentally in a gunfight. Seeing no other option, he crawled back to the doorway and slipped an edge of his body around so that he could get a good view of the onrushing Fergus.

"Drop it!" he shouted when the man was almost upon him.

Instead, Fergus opened fire. His first errant bullet struck a saddle horse almost sixty yards up the street and took off its right ear. The poor horse reared back, screaming with pain, and busted its reins, then raced up the street, almost trampling a boy in the process.

When Fergus kept firing, Longarm had no choice but to kill the crazy fool. The target was so large that it was easy to put a bullet right in the man's heart, and this Longarm did without hesitation. He supposed he could have winged Fergus, but the man might have managed to get off a couple of more wild bullets and inflict damage on someone, so Longarm just put the ugly, lawman-hating sonofabitch out of his misery.

Fergus was dead before he slid to the boardwalk. His skidding body overturned a big apple barrel in front of the Virginia Street Market. Apples went flying everywhere, and several rolled to a stop beside Fergus's mouth so that he looked like he'd been about to sample one.

"Easy, ladies," Longarm said, turning around to look at the assortment of women, most of them old and almost hysterical, but one of them young, blond, and poker-faced. "The shooting is over."

"Did you kill him?" the young woman asked, stepping outside and then staring at the dead man.

"He gave me no choice," Longarm explained. "Fergus might have killed an innocent bystander."

5

"So I can see," the young woman said. "Why was he trying to kill you?"

"He drank too much bad beer and he hated lawmen."

"And you're a lawman?"

"I am." He removed his hat. Custis Long, deputy United States marshal working out of Denver, Colorado, and soon to be on the next train home."

"Miss Megan Riley," she told him, staring at the dead Fergus with an air of revulsion. "That was an evil man. You have done the citizens of Reno a service, and I'm sure that my father would be the first one to agree."

"Are you Marshal Riley's daughter?"

"I am."

Longarm was aware that a lot of people were starting to emerge from cover and fill the street. He was also aware that he needed to be acting "official" right now despite the fact that Megan was so lovely he was badly distracted.

"Miss Riley," he said, "I had been meaning to visit your father. I understand that he is unwell."

"Very unwell," Megan said. "But I think that you still should have shown him the courtesy of a visit, even if he is retired from his duties. After all, he did save your life once, did he not?"

"No," Longarm replied, "I saved *his* life two years ago."

"That's not the way my father tells it."

"Well," Longarm said, very much wishing to avoid an argument but also wanting to set the record straight, "that's the way it happened. I'm sure there were witnesses, if it's important enough for you to check up on."

"It isn't," Megan said. "But don't you think you had better attend to business instead of arguing with me?"

The woman was right, though it galled Longarm to ad-

6

mit the fact. He removed his hat and wiped his brow of sweat. He raised his hands up toward the increasingly vocal crowd to motion for silence, "Ladies and gentlemen, we had an unfortunate misunderstanding here, but there is—"

"Unfortunate!" an old woman cried. "You shoot down Fergus MacDonald and you call it unfortunate! Why, you murdered the big, dumb beast!"

The woman looked around at her fellow citizens. "Someone needs to arrest this man for murder! Where is our new marshal when you need him!"

"Look!" Longarm shouted with mounting exasperation. "I am a deputy United States marshal and this man was out of control. I *had* to shoot him before he killed or badly wounded some innocent citizen. Now, we'll get this thing all settled, but first we really need an undertaker."

"I'm coming!" a tall, emaciated-looking man in his late fifties cried, racing up to join them.

"That man can *smell* blood!" an older woman with her hat all askew snipped.

"Why, it's Fergus!" the undertaker cried, dropping to the fallen man's side and placing his fingers on the man's neck as if to check his pulse. "And he's dead."

"That's right," Longarm said, watching as the undertaker leaned over Fergus and surreptitiously rifled the bartender's pockets. Apparently he found nothing because he said, "Well, I hope that he has friends who will pay for my services."

"For Chrissakes!" a short, slightly winded man wearing a marshal's badge growled as he hurried over to join them. "Just go in and get a case of his beer in payment."

"That poison? Not on your life," the undertaker hissed.

"What happened?" the marshal demanded, eyes shifting over the crowd of gawkers.

7

Longarm pulled back his coat to reveal his badge, which had been hidden from open view. He rarely displayed the badge except when necessary, firmly convinced that there were too many men with Fergus's disagreeable attitude toward lawmen and inclined toward gun trouble.

"I shot that man in self-defense," Longarm explained.

The marshal studied Longarm for a moment as if he could detect truth or guilt. Finally, he looked around at the others and said, "Any witnesses among you that actually saw the shooting?"

"I did," Megan answered as she took a step forward, detaching herself from the excited crowd.

"You did not!" one of the older women argued. "I swear that you were ducking and hiding just like the rest of us!"

"I ducked, sure," Megan said, blue eyes flashing. "But I kept my eyes on Marshal Long, and I heard Fergus shooting long before this brave man stepped outside and put one through the bartender's heart."

"You're sure of that?" the marshal asked, gaze shifting back and forth between the girl and Longarm.

"Of course I am!" Megan said angrily. "Why are you making such a big damned deal out of a lawman defending his own life! Marshal Rouse, my father wouldn't waste a minute asking such dumb questions."

Rouse colored with embarrassment. "Your father did things his way. I do them by the book."

Rouse turned to Longarm and said, "I'm going to need you to write out a statement describing what happened. And then Judge Leroy Potter will most certainly want to have a private word with you."

"Sorry, but I got a train to catch in about . . ." Longarm consulted his watch. "About twenty minutes."

"I'm sorry too," the marshal said, "because you're not

leaving my town until we've got all the loose ends of this tied up. A man—a taxpaying citizen of Reno—has been shot down in the street, and I'm sure that you understand that we're not going to let you waltz out of town until we've filled out all the reports and completely satisfied ourselves that everything is in proper order.''

"Proper order?" Longarm bristled. "Listen! I've got a train to catch, and I'll be damned if I'm going to hang around here an extra couple of days so that I can cross the t's and dot the i's in your damned statement."

Marshal Rouse tried to bluster, but failed and swallowed loudly. "Listen," he said, his voice becoming more conciliatory, "why don't we hurry on over to the office and take care of this right now? I'm sure that, if Miss Riley will cooperate and fill out a similar statement, we can—"

"I'm not filling out anything!" Megan stated. "Marshal Rouse, I told you that I heard that horrid man shooting at Marshal Long and that I saw him fire one returning shot in self-defense. That ought to be plenty good enough for you, and I won't waste my time on anything more."

"My sentiments exactly," Longarm said. "This whole thing is a bunch of nonsense."

Rouse looked pained, but was smart enough to say, "All right, dammit! Just scribble a couple of notes! You can both trouble yourselves that much, can't you?"

Longarm took a deep breath, then expelled it slowly. Having been a lawman for quite some time, he could see that this new marshal was losing face in front of the townspeople and now was reduced to practically begging. Longarm was not an unreasonable man, and took pity.

"Very well," he said. "I'll scratch out a few sentences."

"Thank you," Marshal Rouse said, looking extremely

9

relieved. "And never mind about seeing the judge. I'll explain that you were needed somewhere else."

The marshal turned to Megan and tried to smile, but didn't quite succeed. "Miss Riley, I know that you don't have much respect for me . . ."

"At least you've got that much right."

". . . but if you would just try and cooperate, just a little, we can have all of this settled in a very few minutes and the marshal can be on that train. Won't you please try and be reasonable?"

Megan relented. "Very well. But let's hurry up. I've got an engagement to keep."

"Thank you." Rouse drew a dirty handkerchief out of his back pocket and mopped his perspiring face. He looked very nervous and upset when he said to Longarm and Megan, "Would you both please come along?"

Longarm offered Megan Riley the crook of his arm while saying, "I'm obliged to you for this inconvenience, miss."

"It's worth it to see Fergus finally get what he had coming for a lot of years. My father should have shot the bastard years ago and done everyone in this town a service."

Longarm was shocked at Megan's rough and seemingly callous language, but then realized that he shouldn't have been. Old Marshal Bill Riley had been a heller and had always sworn like a mule skinner. It was small wonder that his daughter possessed a sharp tongue.

When they reached the marshal's little office, they were ushered inside and directed to a pair of scarred old desks. Marshal Rouse was nervous and in a hurry.

"Here," he said, extending pads to them both, "just write down a few paragraphs describing the events that took place and then sign your names."

"Damned foolishness, this," Megan groused.

"You're right," Longarm agreed.

Just then, Longarm heard the shrill and unmistakable sound of a distant and approaching train whistle. He bent over the pad of paper and began to scribble.

His statement was brief, hastily written, and no doubt riddled with hurried misspellings. Longarm did not care. He stated in his long, flowing script that he had been forced to defend himself, first in the saloon, then later outside when Fergus MacDonald had attempted to shoot him in the back as he was walking down the boardwalk.

"This ought to do it," Longarm said, laying his pen down and coming to his feet. "Now, if you'll excuse me, there's that train to catch."

"Don't worry," Rouse said. "The train has to take on wood and water and also new passengers after the ones from Sacramento disembark. I promise that your train will be here for at least forty minutes, and probably an hour."

Longarm sat back down while Rouse read the hastily composed statement. When the marshal of Reno looked up, he was frowning. "You're rather blunt with your words, aren't you."

"I say what I mean," Longarm growled. "Paperwork isn't my long suit, but I expect you're a real whiz at it."

Rouse blushed. "I guess you think you've just insulted me, but the fact of the matter is that I do take considerable pride in the work that I do. Reports are very important."

"Oh, bullshit," Megan said, finishing her own statement.

"It's the truth," Rouse persisted. "And that's one of the reasons why Marshal Riley needed to retire."

Megan's blue eyes flashed. "That's a lie! He retired because he's old and his eyesight failed him. Otherwise, he'd still be in this office and you'd still be a miserable,

11

second-rate little clerk in at the Wells Fargo Bank.''

Rouse shook with pent-up anger. ''You've a bad habit of speaking without thinking, young woman.''

Megan came to her feet, then stomped toward the door, where she turned and shouted, ''You're out of your element, Rouse. Someone is going to shoot you down or run you out of town with your tail tucked between your legs. You don't have the ability, the courage, or the brains to be a lawman.''

''Why, you—!''

But Megan was already stomping outside, slamming the door behind her.

''Sonofabitch!'' Rouse shouted hoarsely. ''That woman needs a good whipping!''

Longarm was amused. ''Well,'' he said, ''she does have a sharp tongue and a lively way about her. But I'd say that you're not the one to put Miss Riley in her place. Hell, Marshal, I think she'd whip you in a flash.''

Rouse looked ready to explode with anger when Longarm excused himself and went out the door with a chuckle.

''Well,'' Rouse said, heading out the door too, ''we'll just see how smart-assed you really are after I talk to Judge Potter and he summons you to his chambers!''

It was a surprisingly short hour later when Marshal Rouse boarded the waiting train out of breath but wearing a look of triumph on his round, sweaty face.

''Marshal Long,'' he said formally as he found Longarm reclining in a coach seat, ''I'm afraid that Judge Potter has summoned you for further questioning.''

''What!''

''That's right,'' Rouse said, barely able to suppress a

12

grin. "I have his subpoena right here in my hand. Would you come along, please."

"Hell, no!"

Rouse's smile turned nasty. "I had anticipated that you would be uncooperative and took the liberty of sending a telegram to your superior in Denver."

"You telegraphed Billy Vail?"

"I did and he sent an immediate rely." Rouse extended the telegram. It read simply:

CUSTIS COOPERATE STOP

"You low-down, sneaky little sonofabitch," Longarm breathed, crumpling up the telegram and hurling it at the leering marshal as he came to his feet.

"Would you follow me, please," Rouse said almost sweetly as he pivoted on his heels and headed toward the vestibule of the coach.

Longarm was powerfully tempted to ignore Billy's terse telegram, but after a second of indecision, he decided that he had better follow his boss's orders and get this matter settled. He'd miss his train, sure enough, but he did want to see and pay his respects to old Marshal Riley, and he sure wanted to see Megan again.

She was the kind of passionate and strong-willed woman that Longarm found almost irresistible.

Chapter 2

Judge Leroy Potter was a withered and taciturn old man who preferred to wear a silk bathrobe and slippers, even when his court was in session. His face was gaunt, his eyes dull, dark spots in deep sockets, his lips thin, bloodless, and perpetually disapproving.

"So," he said in a weak, raspy voice as he leaned forward, surrounded by walls of his library's books, "did you really think, Mr. Long, that you could kill a man in Reno and then just walk away without an investigation or interrogation?"

"There was a witness," Longarm said pointedly. "Miss—"

"I know, I know," the judge snapped impatiently. "Miss Riley. But she *hated* Fergus MacDonald because the man gave her father so much grief during his later, declining years as our city's marshal."

Longarm decided to keep his opinions private. It was clear that this judge was irritable and mean-spirited. What was not clear was his intention, which, Longarm suspected, would not be good.

"Tell me, in great detail," the judge ordered, "exactly what happened."

"I was walking down the boardwalk and Fergus jumped out. He shouted my name and opened fire. I jumped into the millinery store and warned the customers to stay low and not to panic. Then I eased out the door and shot the man as he came rushing at me firing his pistol and spraying bullets everywhere."

"Why would he do that?"

"He hated lawmen," Longarm said. "MacDonald confessed that to me after we had a minor disagreement in his saloon."

The judge's eyes tightened around the corners. Potter looked as old as an oak, but crafty as an alley cat. "I understand," he said, eyes darting to Rouse, "that you whipped Mr. MacDonald quite viciously."

"Nothing could be further from the truth," Longarm retorted hotly. "In fact, I only hit him three times, once in the gut and twice more in the kidneys. After that, Fergus said he'd had enough and I walked away."

"There are witnesses that said Mr. MacDonald was spitting up blood as he ran down the boardwalk after you. That he looked as if he was dying."

"That's ridiculous!" Longarm took a deep, steadying breath. "I'll grant you, Judge, that I hit the man hard. There was no choice because he was big and strong. And maybe a couple of hard shots to the kidneys will cause a man to spit up a little blood, but I assure you that Fergus MacDonald was not dying on account of my blows."

"That remains to be seen," the judge snapped.

"What are you driving at?" Longarm demanded.

"Simply that I have ordered an autopsy," the judge said. "One that will allow us to complete a full report on this matter."

"Are you saying that you think I was somehow at fault? That I shouldn't have killed Fergus MacDonald

16

even though he'd already shot a horse and was wild enough to have shot innocent bystanders?''

The judge's eyes grew frosty. ''I don't like your attitude, Marshal Long. You seem to be a little too quick to kill a man. You should have left that saloon and lodged a written complaint with Marshal Rouse.''

''A *written* complaint?'' Longarm asked, hardly believing he'd heard correctly. ''Judge, surely you jest!''

The judge, however, wasn't jesting. His face paled and his thin, heavily veined hands palsied with agitation. ''I am just about to have you jailed for contempt of my court!''

''This isn't a court!''

Judge Potter snapped. He jumped up and pointed a bony finger at Longarm, then screeched, ''Marshal Rouse, arrest this man!''

Longarm took a backward step. ''Now wait a minute,'' he said, shaking his head. ''I'm a *federal* officer of the law, and I will not be arrested on the order of some senile old judge who should have been forcibly retired from the bench years ago.''

''Arrest him!'' Potter shrieked, spittle flying from his mouth. ''Arrest this man and lock him up in jail!''

Longarm didn't want to defy the local authorities, but enough was enough. He turned toward Marshal Rouse and there was a hard warning in his voice when he said, ''Don't even try. I'm sick and tired of this farce and I'm not about to go to jail.''

''You're breaking the law,'' Rouse said, his voice reedy with nervousness. ''If you submit, I'm sure that His Honor will soon turn you loose.''

''To hell with His Honor!''

''Arrest him!'' Potter screamed again.

''Try it,'' Longarm warned, ''and you'll be sorry.''

Potter jumped to his feet, almost losing his balance and spilling to the floor. He began screaming obscenities. Marshal Rouse looked terrified, probably even more so of the judge than of Longarm.

"I'll have you thrown in prison!" Potter sputtered, finally collapsing back into his chair.

"No, you won't," Longarm said. "You're just a sick, twisted old man and I'm going to pull whatever strings I can to see that you are removed from the bench. Frankly, I think you are mentally unstable."

Potter went insane. He jumped to his feet, took two steps toward Longarm with outstretched hands, and then pitched forward with a gasp and then a cry of pain.

"Oh, God!" Rouse cried. "He's having another stroke!"

"Another . . ."

Longarm dropped to his knees and rolled the old man over. Potter was turning blue, and then his frail little body stiffened and his head shook violently back and forth a moment before he went completely limp as his final breath wheezed from his lungs.

"He's dead!" Rouse cried, looking stunned. "Judge Potter is really dead!"

Longarm felt for a pulse. "Yep," he said with a barely suppressed grin, "the mean old bastard is finally dead and now *he's* the one who will be judged."

Rouse staggered backward and puddled into a chair. "I need a drink," he whispered, pointing vaguely toward the judge's fully stocked liquor cabinet.

Longarm marched over to the cabinet, found a flask of what looked to be rye whiskey, and poured them both glasses.

"Salute!" he said gravely, handing the marshal a brimming full glass.

"Salute," Rouse replied in a subdued tone of voice.

They drank, emptying their glasses, and when Rouse signaled he wanted a refill, Longarm thought, *What the hell, why not?*

They drank several more rounds.

"Sorry you missed your train," Rouse finally offered.

"That's all right," Longarm said, taking a cheroot from his pocket and stuffing it into his mouth. "Wasn't your fault, exactly."

"Thanks. I guess you aren't too used to putting up with paperwork, huh?" Rouse said cautiously.

"Oh," Longarm mused, splitting the last of the whiskey between them. "I've got my share of paperwork to do, but I sure never took statements when someone shot someone else in order to protect their life."

"Judge Potter was a stickler for that," Rouse said, his voice thickening as he stared at the dead man. "I guess now I'm probably going to have to leave this job."

"How'd you get it in the first place?" Longarm asked. "I mean, no offense, but you don't really seem to be cut to the mold of a lawman."

"Well, I'd have to agree with that," Rouse said. "Mainly, I just was trying to impress a town girl. But she married someone else anyway, so I guess that didn't work."

"I guess not," Longarm agreed. "And speaking of girls, where does Miss Riley live?"

At the mention of her name, Rouse's nose wrinkled with disgust. "You don't want anything to do with *her*!"

"I take it that you don't exactly hold each other in high regard."

"You could say that again," Rouse snapped. "She thinks I'm worse than dog-shit!"

"Naw."

"It's true!" Rouse exclaimed. "But it's also true that no man could fill the job that her pa was forced out of because he got too old and blind. To her, Old Wild Bill Riley will always be the finest lawman that ever lived."

"Well," Longarm sympathized, "I can see how that could easily happen. But I'd still like to pay Miss Riley and her father a visit. He used to be a real fine lawman and we got along very well."

"The old devil lives just south of town. Big ranch house with a front porch and a rooster weather vane on the barn. It's faded brown, and there's a tall cottonwood out front with a kid's swing attached to it."

"Megan's kid?"

"Naw," Rouse said, "it's just some kid that lived there before 'em and they never took it down. Bill Riley isn't the kind of a man who puts much value in appearances, as you are probably aware."

"Yes," Longarm said, "I am aware of that. What does his daughter do?"

"She's a worker," Rouse admitted. "She breaks horses, mostly, but she also mends saddles and such."

"That's unusual for a woman."

"She looks like a woman, but she swears like a ranch hand and she's tougher than rawhide," Rouse warned. "I tell you, if a man tried her on, he'd be in for a rough, rough ride!"

Longarm didn't appreciate that comment, but Rouse was pretty drunk and obviously he'd considered the judge a friend, so Longarm guessed he'd let the crude comment pass. "Well, I guess I'll go see them. How far south of town is the Riley place?"

"About a mile." Rouse shook his head looking completely demoralized. "I guess I better go get the undertaker. Barney is going to be a happy man today, what

20

with two bodies hitting the slabs at the same time. Everyone knows that old Judge Potter had a lot of money, and Barney will charge plenty to bury him and really put on the dog. Flowers. Big marble headstone with lots of poetry and carved angels and vines. You know, just everything including polishing up the big hearse and renting a pair of matched white horses.''

''I've seen it all, but I expect,'' Longarm said, ''that Fergus's funeral will be a little less impressive.''

''Oh, I wouldn't say that. Every man and woman in Reno hated Fergus MacDonald so much I'm sure that they'll all come to see him planted.'' Rouse sighed. ''I'll have to agree with Megan that killing him was a blessing for our town.''

Longarm headed briskly for the door, but when he stepped out onto the judge's porch, the heat made his head spin a little.

''Whew!'' he exhaled. ''Is it ever going to cool down?''

''I sure hope so,'' Rouse said, coming outside to join him. ''But old Barney is going to have to plant both the judge and Fergus tomorrow or they'll raise quite a stink.''

''I expect so,'' Longarm said, squinting and heading for the livery to rent a horse.

He rode up to the Riley place less than an hour later on a sorry-looking strawberry roan horse that only cost him a dollar to rent for the remainder of the day. Dismounting, Longarm tied the pathetic, swaybacked beast to the cottonwood tree and marched up to the front door. Banging it hard, he yelled, ''Hey, Bill! It's me, Custis Long!''

Longarm heard the unmistakable cocking of a gun hammer, and he retreated off the porch shouting, ''Bill, dammit, it's Custis Long! You remember me, the federal marshal from Denver that saved your bacon about two years back.''

A moment of silence, and then the door eased open a crack and Wild Bill Riley appeared. Longarm barely recognized the old lawman. Bill was down to skin and bone. He was wearing coveralls without an undershirt, and his bare arms were wasted with hardly any muscle. Only the steadiness of his gun hand was a reminder of the man who had once been sensationalized in a dime novel as ''the last of the great gun-totin' marshals.''

He squinted, waved his six-gun around, and said, ''That really you, Custis?''

Longarm relaxed. ''Damn right it is! How the hell are you, Wild Bill!''

''Not so wild anymore,'' Bill Riley said, a half-smile on his face. ''Can barely find and hoist my dick anymore.''

Longarm chuckled. ''The next thing I know, you'll be telling me that you can't hit the side of a barn with that old six-shooter. But I know that isn't true.''

''I expect not,'' Bill said, '' 'cause I can hit what I can hear and my ears still work fine. Come on inside and get outa that damned heat.''

Longarm was only too happy to do that. He followed Bill inside the dim room, noting that the furniture was worn but comfortable.

''Custis, find yourself a chair and tell me what brings you here,'' Bill ordered.

Longarm sat down, feeling a pounding in his skull due to the whiskey he'd shared with Rouse. He quickly sketched in what had happened back in Reno, and when he was finished, Bill was grinning like an old fool.

''So you killed Fergus MacDonald, huh?''

''Had no choice.''

"And then you rattled Judge Potter so bad that he had a stroke, huh?"

"Wasn't anything I set out to do," Longarm said defensively. "I didn't have any way of knowing that he had a bad ticker."

"Jeezus," the old man chuckled. "You blow into town and are responsible for the deaths of two sonsabitches that I wanted to kill for years! How the hell do you get things done so fast?"

Longarm shook his head. "The last thing I want is trouble, but it has a way of dogging me wherever I go."

"You draw out the worst in men," Bill said. "I wouldn't worry about that too much, though."

"I don't." Longarm looked around the interior of the ranch house. The furniture was worn, but of good quality, and he could see a woman's touch in the curtains and in the fact that there were pictures on the walls. "Where's your daughter?"

"I'm just not sure. She had to dress up and go shopping with Mrs. Else Peterson, who has some horses that needed breaking. My daughter hates to wear a dress and try to look like a lady, but I sure enjoy seeing her gussied up once in a while."

"She was in the millinery store when Fergus came gunning for me. I thought she'd probably have come back here and told you all about it."

"Nope. Most likely, Megan's down at Mrs. Peterson's place, riding fancy horses for that rich old lady. Nothing that Megan would rather do than to be on horseback."

"I see," Longarm said, trying to hide his disappointment. "Does she generally come back to cook your meal after she finishes with the horses?"

"Nope," Bill said, "I cook for *her*." He winked. "Do

23

you still want to stay for supper?"

"I guess so."

"Good! I've got a pot of beans and soda bread I'm heating up for tonight."

"Sounds delicious," Longarm said, mustering up every last bit of enthusiasm.

Bill hobbled over to the couch and removed a cushion, then stuck his skinny arm down inside the overstuffed piece of furniture. When he pulled it free, he was holding a full bottle of whiskey.

"This is what sounds delicious," Bill corrected. "And it's what will make my beans and soda bread edible."

Longarm really didn't feel like he needed anything more to drink this day. In fact, he was just starting to sober up good, but it didn't seem very neighborly to decline to drink with Old Wild Bill Riley, so he took his glass and they toasted.

"To blood and bullets," Bill crowed.

"To blood and bullets," Longarm repeated before touching the glass to his lips.

Two hours later, the beans and the bread were scorched and burned and Megan waltzed in the door wearing a man's shirt and pants. She was dressed like a bronc buster with boots and spurs, and her face was covered with grit and her pretty hair was pulled back tight.

"Well, hello, darlin'!" Bill called.

Megan's blue eyes went icy as she studied her father, then Longarm. After a moment of silence, she said, "Marshal, everyone in Reno is talking about you. Some say you caused the death of old Judge Potter, some say not. Which is it?"

"I guess I got him pretty upset and nature did the rest," Longarm replied, trying very hard not to look pleased with himself.

"In that case, pour me a glass of whiskey and I'll raise a toast to you for killing the two orneriest sonsabitches in town."

Longarm grinned loosely. "Yes, ma'am!"

"Now don't you go lookin' at my girl thataway!" Bill said with a wink. "Or I'll get out my whittlin' knife and make sure you don't ever come back here again."

Longarm blushed, but the old man cackled and even Megan had to laugh.

"Pa! Did you burn the damned beans and bread again?"

"Afraid so."

"Shit!" Megan stormed, marching over to the water pump by the kitchen sink and washing her hands, then her face. "I guess I'm going to have to go out in the cooler and cut us some pork off that butcher hog."

She looked at Longarm. "That all right with you? It isn't too green yet."

"Sure," he said, not sure if she was joshing him or if it was the truth and his gut would soon have to contend not only with too much whiskey but also bad pork.

"Good," Megan said, grabbing a big butcher knife and disappearing through the door.

"Hell of a girl," Bill said, a droopy smile on his lips. "Don't know what I'd do without her."

"I'll bet."

Less than five minutes later, Megan reappeared carrying a slab of pork, and damned if it didn't have a greenish look to it.

"Be ready before you know it!" she called.

"Take your time," Longarm said. "No hurry at all."

25

Chapter 3

By nine o'clock that evening, Wild Bill had fallen asleep and was snoring heavily. As a result of the cooking, it was quite hot in the Riley house and Longarm, working on a full stomach and too much whiskey, knew that he had to go outdoors and get some fresh air before he also started to nod off.

"Would you like to go for a walk?" he said to Megan. "I could use the air and the exercise."

"Sure," she replied. "What about that sorry excuse for a horse you've got tied outside?"

"We can lead him back into town."

"But after that, where are you staying tonight?"

"I don't know," Longarm said.

Megan blinked. "Well, what about your bags? You must have some extra clothes and things."

"I do," Longarm said. "But they were supposed to be put on the eastbound train. I sure hope that the station-master had the good sense to keep my things and not send them east."

"There's always a telegraph operator on duty," Megan said. "We could walk back into town and ask him. He'll have a key to the baggage room and you could get your things.''

''That's a good idea.'' Longarm glanced at Bill. ''He'll be all right?''

''Yes. He's had too much to drink, like he does most every night, but he'll sleep well. He's in considerable pain, you know.''

''No,'' Longarm said. ''He never said anything about it.''

''He's got a cancer,'' Megan said, her eyes misting. ''His drinking doesn't help.''

''I'm sorry.''

''Come on,'' Megan said, heading outside, ''let's get that fresh air we both need.''

Longarm untied his livery horse, and then they all walked along in silence toward the town until they came to the livery. Longarm unsaddled the poor horse and then turned it loose in an empty corral.

They couldn't leave until Megan was satisfied that the poor beast had plenty of hay and water. ''Even an ugly horse deserves good treatment,'' she explained. ''After all, it can't help the way it looks any more than we can.''

''I suspect that's so,'' Longarm said.

They continued on into town, and when they reached the Truckee River bridge, Megan stopped and picked up a pebble and threw it into the river. The surface of the water was burnished like copper in the moonlight, and they watched the ripple spread out across the surface, slow and lazy.

''A penny for your thoughts, Megan.''

Stirred from her reverie, she turned and looked at him. ''I was thinking of you, actually.''

Longarm grinned. ''Good.''

''No,'' she said, ''not good. I was wondering if you

will wind up like my father. Old and discarded. A man whose memories haunt him and who wonders if God in heaven will judge him harshly for all those that he has killed.''

Longarm took a deep breath. "If you're talking about men like Fergus MacDonald, I'll take my chances," Longarm said. "I'm not a bit worried about the killing I've done because I've never killed except in the line of duty when every other alternative failed."

Megan turned to Longarm. "I know that," she said softly.

"It's always amazed me that some men like you and my father could deal with so much violence and still retain your decency. Your job requires that you see the very worst in people."

"Sometimes the best," Longarm said. "I've seen a lot of courage and sacrifice. I'm sure that your father has also told you of the many acts of bravery he's witnessed."

"He has."

"Megan, what will you do when he's gone?"

She didn't hesitate. "I'll do what I've been doing. Nothing much will change, except that I won't have a man to burn meat for and to tease a little the way I do with father. I'll keep on working with horses and leather."

"I don't hear any talk of a husband and children."

"I've never thought much about them one way or the other," she admitted. Then she smiled and added, "When I was a girl, I had a few beaus come by to pay their respects."

"As pretty as you are, more than a few, I'll wager."

Megan didn't deny it. "But Old Wild Bill ran them all off. He'd let them in the house, but then he'd get drunk and rowdy and scare 'em half to death. They never came back again. After a while, the word got around to all the

29

young men and they just stopped paying their visits.''

"You're still a young woman.''

"I am,'' she agreed, "but I'm pretty stubborn and set in my ways. I'm not sure that any man could put up with me. He'd have to be a horseman, of course.''

"Of course.''

"I'd never marry a merchant or someone like that.''

"No,'' Longarm said, "that would never work.''

"I'd want a man like my father, but one not quite so demanding. He was tough on my mother. I can remember that he bossed her around something fierce.''

"I can well imagine that he would.''

Megan's eyes narrowed and she grew very serious. "I won't be bossed around, Custis. If someone pushes me into a corner, I get mad and want to fight. You can't order me around and treat me like I'm some second-class citizen.''

"Of course not.''

Megan picked up another pebble and tossed it over the bridge toward the tules where a bullfrog was raising a ruckus. The bullfrog splashed away and the night grew still again, except for the sounds of laughter and music that floated out of the Virginia Street saloons.

"But I'd want a strong man,'' Megan said, talking to the water below. "For all his faults, my father was always strong and I can't abide weaklings.''

"Have you ever even had a man?'' Longarm asked quietly.

Megan sighed, and it was a long time before she said, "I don't know whether to haul off and slap you or to truthfully answer your question.''

"You just answered it,'' he said, pulling her tight against his chest. "You're a virgin, aren't you?''

She gulped. "I guess there's nothing wrong with that, even at my age."

"How old are you?"

"Twenty-four."

"There's nothing wrong with being a virgin at any age," he told her in his gentlest voice. "All it means is that you haven't met the right man."

"Are you thinking you are the right man?"

"No," he said.

Megan blinked, and Longarm knew his answer had caught her by surprise. "You aren't?"

"No."

"Then . . ."

Longarm kissed her mouth. Megan's didn't resist, but she clearly was unsure of herself and hadn't had any practice in kissing. Her mouth was closed tight and her lips were unresponsive.

"Relax," he whispered. "Just enjoy the feel of it."

"I'm not sure that's the wise thing to do," she told him. "And anyway, what if someone sees us?"

"That wouldn't be the end of the world either," he said. "Now would it?"

In answer, Megan pressed her mouth tighter to his own and clung to him. She was strong, smelled of horse and sweat, but was still someone extremely desirable. Longarm could feel his loins stir, and his pulse began to race.

"Maybe," he said a moment later, "we should *both* find a place for the night."

"No," she panted, recoiling. "I . . . I don't think that would be such a good idea."

"Why not?"

"Because I might like it too much, and then you'd be leaving for Denver and where would I be?"

"You'd be fine," he assured her. "You'd start thinking

31

about a husband . . . just the kind that you described. And then maybe even children some day.''

''I don't think I want children, and I'm not even sure I want a husband. I like horses best.''

Longarm couldn't help himself. He laughed despite the seriousness in Megan, and then he said, ''That could change over time, Megan.''

''I hope not.''

''Come on,'' he said, taking her arm and heading across the bridge. ''Let's find out if my baggage is on its way to Cheyenne or if the stationmaster was sharp enough to keep it here for me.''

Megan smiled up at Longarm and said, ''I'll bet I'm the worst kisser you ever kissed, huh?''

''Not *the* worst,'' he said teasingly, ''but you do have a ways to go.''

''Like what should I do different?''

''Relax and enjoy how it makes you feel.''

''And what if it ever makes me feel pukey?''

Longarm barked a laugh. ''That's a surefire sign that you're kissing someone that you shouldn't.''

Megan marched along beside him a few more steps, then looked up and blurted out. ''Kissing you makes my toes curl and my insides feel weak.''

''Hmmm. Anything else?''

''Made . . . never mind.''

He looked down at her. ''I got an idea what it did to you, Megan. And you had just better watch yourself or you'll get to liking it and even wanting more.''

''Like a mare in heat, huh?''

''Something like that, but with all kinds of other things going on in your head and your heart.''

''Sounds to me like it could really mess a girl up.''

"It can, and it does when you get involved with the wrong kind of man."

Megan didn't say anything more after that. Longarm had given her plenty to think about, and she looked both excited and worried when they stepped onto the train station platform and then entered the station itself.

"Good evening," a lone figure seated beside a telegrapher's keys said. "Can I help you?"

"I hope so," Longarm said, quickly explaining about his baggage. "I'm here to see if you've still got it or if it's mistakenly been sent east."

The telegrapher, a thin, balding man in his mid-forties with wire-rimmed spectacles, stood up and reached for a key that was hanging on the wall. "And your name?"

"Long. Deputy United States Marshal Custis Long."

The telegrapher smiled. "Oh, yes. Marshal Long. Not only have we retained your baggage, but I have a very important telegram for you. Figured you'd come around soon enough."

He turned to Megan with a warm smile. "Top of the evenin', Miss Riley."

"Evening, Carl."

"Now," Carl said. "Which do you want first? The telegram or the baggage?"

"I know what I've got in my bags, but I sure am curious about that telegram. I guess it's the second one I received today."

"Yes," Carl said, "the first one was pretty short, wasn't it."

"It was."

Carl rummaged around in a file and then retrieved the new telegram, which Longarm read immediately.

BIG TROUBLE IN BODIE STOP KANES
MAYBE GONE BAD STOP UNOFFICIALLY

"What's wrong?" Megan asked.

"There's some trouble in Bodie that I have to take care of," Longarm said, thinking about Ivan Kane and judging he had not seen the old lawman in a good dozen years. Kane was a legend in the West, but like Wild Bill Riley, a man past his time. He'd started out as an outlaw and then had gone to prison, but had come out reformed and determined to redeem himself. And had he ever! Kane had become a one-man crusader against lawlessness, first in the California gold fields, and then on the Comstock Lode and in a slew of other notorious Nevada and Arizona mining towns.

"I know Marshal Kane personally," the telegraph operator said. "And it disturbs me to hear the talk about what he's been doing down in Bodie."

"What exactly has he been accused of doing?"

Carl sighed. "They say he's become more than a lawman. They say he is too quick on the trigger and ready to shoot down anyone who so much as looks crossways at him."

"He always had a short fuse," Longarm agreed, "but he's not bloodthirsty."

"He might have become that way," Carl said, clucking his tongue. "I'm sure that you realize that power . . . real power . . . corrupts the morals of even the strongest man. Marshal Kane has ruled Bodie for at least eight or nine years. When the town fathers hired him to clean out the bad element, he did it without a badge, and anyone will tell you that he basically ambushed and backshot the outlaws. Those that he didn't kill fled. Furthermore, we hear that he's extorting protection money from Bodie's mer-

34

chants, mine owners, and professional people.''

"That can't be true!'' Megan exclaimed. "My father and Marshal Kane have been friends for the last twenty-five years. Kane is tough, but honest.''

"Well,'' Carl said, "if you throw a good apple in a barrel of bad, it'll turn rotten too. What I hear is that the good people of Bodie are about ready to do Marshal Kane in, one way or the other.''

"I'd better head out for Bodie first thing in the morning,'' Longarm said. "Carl, when is the next eastbound train leaving?''

"Next Monday at three in the afternoon. The train after that leaves a week from today, same as always.''

"I'll need at least a full week to 'unofficially' wrap this up,'' Longarm said.

"I'm coming with you,'' Megan announced.

"No,'' Longarm said, "your father needs you here.''

"The next house down from us is owned by an old widow woman named Mrs. Appleton. She'll look in on Father and feed him better than I could. He'll be happy because he has sort of taken a shine to her since he found out she's got a lot of money in the bank.''

"What would your father do with the money if—''

"I don't know,'' Megan interrupted. "He can't take it with him. But anyway, I'm coming.''

"That's okay with me as long as it's okay with your father. I sure don't want Wild Bill after my hide. I'm going to have enough trouble in Bodie.''

"You want your baggage now?'' Carl asked.

"That'd be good,'' Longarm said.

In a few minutes, he had his baggage and they were trudging back down Virginia Street.

"Where are you going to stay tonight?'' she asked a little shyly.

35

"How about at your place, Megan?"

"Sure," she agreed. "I'll pitch some fresh straw in a stall and you'll be plenty comfortable."

"That's not exactly what I had in mind," he told her.

"I know, but we can talk about that on the way to Bodie."

Longarm grinned. "At least now I'll have something to look forward to."

Megan shot him a look that held a lot of promise, and she hugged his arm. Boy, Longarm thought, what I wouldn't give to have this lusty virgin in the hay tonight!

Chapter 4

Early the next morning, Longarm, still half asleep and covered with wisps of straw, was awakened by Megan, who stood before him looking bright-eyed and holding a cup of steaming-hot coffee.

"Rise and shine, Marshal Long!" she said, kneeling down beside him and extending the cup.

Longarm raised one droopy eyelid and glared at her. He could see but a faint light shafting through the rafters of the barn. "What time is it?"

"Five-thirty," Megan announced.

"Jeezus," Longarm moaned. "What's the big hurry?"

"It's better than a hundred miles to Bodie, and some of it is pretty rough traveling. We need to get a move on if we're going to get into California by tonight."

"I take it you've some pretty decent saddle horses?"

"About a thousand times better than the one you rented yesterday," she replied. "I love *all* horses, but I only own horses of quality."

"All right," Longarm said, taking a sip of the coffee. "Why don't you go along and I'll come up to the house in a few minutes after I've sort of gathered my wits."

"That's fine. Father and I have been up for an hour and he's got breakfast about ready."

"You people are really something. By the way, what did Old Wild Bill say when you told him that you were planning to accompany me to Bodie?"

Megan squatted down on her boot heels. She looked young and eager and prettier than any woman had a right to be at this awful hour in the morning. Right now, however, her blue eyes reflected worry.

"Well, my father wasn't too happy about the idea," Megan admitted with a sigh of resignation. "In fact, when I woke him up this morning and told him that I was leaving with you, he was pretty damned mad."

"I'll bet." Longarm blew steam from the coffee. It was almost scalding hot. "And now he's going to be mad at me because he'll think it was all my idea."

"No he won't," Megan said quickly. "I made it clear that the whole thing was my idea. I told him that there were some horses in Bodie that needed breaking and that could perhaps be bought and resold at a hefty profit."

Longarm had been about to take another sip, but now he stopped, cup frozen near his lips. "You told him that you were going along with me to break and perhaps buy some Bodie horses?"

"Sure."

"But that's a damn lie."

"Maybe not. I do buy problem horses, straighten them out, and resell them for a profit. Besides, look at it this way, Custis. It's far better for me to lie than to have him charge out here and maybe beat you half to death with a singletree. Wouldn't you agree?"

"I sure would," Longarm said, "but I don't want to have to face the man when you come back without any money or horses."

"I'll figure out something." Megan stood up to leave. "Besides, quite honestly, my father is looking forward to Mrs. Appleton coming by to feed and flatter him. She still laughs at his jokes, even the dirty ones, and I think he'd like to seduce her on our kitchen table."

"Old lecher."

"He is," Megan said with a shake of her head. "Sometimes he and Mrs. Appleton get to laughing so hard it darn near sets our dog to howling."

After saying that, Megan went back to the house while Longarm finished his coffee and then batted the straw off himself and shuffled over to a water trough to wash his face, neck, and hands. He combed his hair with his fingers, and found his gunbelt and buckled it on.

Standing in the doorway of the barn, he stretched and then decided he had better get to the table before Bill got upset because of his tardiness.

"Well goddammit!" Bill bellowed in anger, turning away from the stove with a plate of flapjacks in his left hand. "It's just about damn time you showed. I was about to go out there and jerk you right out of your wet dreams."

"Father!" Megan exclaimed. "Behave yourself."

"Sit down, the both of you," Bill ordered.

Longarm glanced at Megan, who indicated that they had better do as her father commanded. For the next few minutes, Bill slammed food down in front of them. Flapjacks, bacon, and fried potatoes along with more coffee.

"Eat up!" the old man exclaimed. "Who knows when you'll eat a decent meal again between here and Bodie."

"You know that there are stage stops along the way where we can eat and rest."

Bill glared at his daughter. "Yeah? And what about where you will sleep?" he challenged.

"So," Longarm said, "is *that* why you're so on the prod this morning?"

"That and a hammer banging me right behind the eyes."

"I keep telling you not to drink so much," Megan said.

"Shut up, girl!"

Bill marched over to loom above Longarm, who was still seated at the table. And though he was old, Wild Bill looked menacing this morning, especially with a coffeepot in his fist.

"You better not diddle around with my daughter, Marshal Long," he warned, coffeepot shaking in his hand. "Because if I ever find out that you've taken advantage of my Megan, I'll shoot your balls off!"

Longarm jumped to his feet. Frankly, his own head was pounding a little. Furthermore, he was stiff from sleeping on the ground, straw or no straw. And finally, he had never been a man who tolerated physical threats, especially the first thing in the morning when he was still half asleep.

"Look here, you old reprobate!" Longarm shouted. "I didn't ask your daughter to come along, she invited herself. And furthermore, I'm not going to take advantage of anyone. I never have and I never will." Longarm's jaw jutted out. He was bigger than Wild Bill and he was armed. "So don't go threatening me, old man."

Bill took a step back, and the purple veins at his temples were visibly throbbing. But at least his voice was several octaves lower when he said, "You just better treat her like a lady. That's all I got to say. If I hear that you weren't a gentleman, I *will* shoot your balls off."

"Is that before or after you screw old giggly Mrs. Appleton on this kitchen table?" Longarm said dryly.

Bill's jaw sagged and his eyes bugged. Longarm braced

himself for a cyclone, but then Bill burst out in laughter. "Goddammit! Did Megan tell you that's what I intend to do to Mrs. Appleton?"

"Yes."

"Shit!" Bill stormed, turning on his daughter but unable to look upset. "You ain't supposed to tell everyone everything I say!"

"Custis isn't everyone," Megan said, relaxing. "Besides, it's the truth. You *did* say that, and you'd be lying if you claimed otherwise."

Bill refilled their cups and sat down. "All right," he said, "you got me. I'm the pot calling the kettle black. Only Mrs. Appleton ain't no virgin and Megan is."

"How do you know that?" Megan asked innocently.

Bill gaped, and then he stammered for words. "You mean . . . who the hell have you been with!"

"No one," she said. "But it could happen some day, and I'll not have you putting a chastity belt around me— in fact or in your dirty old mind. Is that clear, Father?"

Longarm dipped his chin and started shoveling in the food. He did not want to be a part of this family dispute, and he was damned glad that Megan hadn't allowed him to take her to some hotel room last night.

The rest of the conversation was strained and mostly conducted with a series of grunts. Longarm couldn't wait to get out of the house and then pack his belongings and saddle the horse that Megan had chosen for him.

"That horse's name is Arthur", she said later. "He's fast, tough, and he never goes lame."

Longarm liked the looks of the sorrel gelding from the first moment he'd laid eyes on the animal. He was tall and deep-chested, with strong, straight legs. His head was refined, and the animal gave the impression of possessing the enviable combination of intelligence, speed, and great stamina. "My guess is that he's a thoroughbred."

"Crossbred," she said. "Mustang and thoroughbred. They're the best kind of horse I've ever owned. The mare I'll be riding is your gelding's sister."

"They are a fine match."

"Maybe we could be too," Megan said, tossing the offhanded comment at him with a grin so bold that it made Longarm's throat go a little dry.

Megan had packed two big saddlebags with food and tied grain behind their cantles. She'd filled two big canteens, and just before they left, Bill came out to give them each Winchesters to put into their saddle boots.

"There's a long story behind them rifles," he said, "but I reckon that you've not got the time I need for the telling. The important thing, Marshal, is that they are oiled, loaded, and shoot straight. Megan, by the way, is probably a better rifle shot than you are."

"Wouldn't surprise me in the least," Longarm said, climbing into the saddle.

"Just take care of each other," Bill said, almost pleading. "If I don't see you back here to board that eastbound within ten days to two weeks, I'll come looking for you both. Is that understood?"

"Yes sir," Longarm said, extending his hand to the former lawman.

They shook, though Bill's grip was no longer strong.

"You be sure and eat everything that Mrs. Appleton puts on your plate," Megan said. "You know you need to put on some weight and how much she likes it when you empty your plate."

"I'm going to try and find out how much she likes some other things I intend to do," Bill said with a lascivious grin.

"Father!"

The old reprobate cackled a laugh, and then Longarm and Megan reined south. As soon as they were out on the road, Megan touched her heels to her mare's flanks and set the animal into a high lope. Longarm would have preferred to have walked a few miles just to get the stiffness out of his body and warm up the horses, but his animal seemed more than eager to gallop.

Up ahead, Megan was riding like a Comanche Indian. Like she had been born in the saddle. She had long, shapely legs and a firm, round little bottom that rocked back and forth in the saddle in a most attractive and eye-catching way. Because of that enticing view, Longarm held his gelding back so he could let his imagination run wild.

And so, despite the early hour and Wild Bill's ominous threats, Longarm couldn't help but smile as they began to gallop toward the Washoe Valley and Carson City just beyond.

Named after Kit Carson and founded in 1858, Carson City had become the state's capital back in 1864. With its impressive silver dome, big granite courthouse, and legislative offices, the town enjoyed a refinement and civility that was entirely lacking in most Western communities. Carson City had never enjoyed the status of a boom town, like Reno when the Union Pacific had come through or when gold had been discovered at Virginia City or Gold Hill. Instead, Carson City had always been content to retain a quiet dignity befitting its role as the seat of Nevada politics. Its wide streets were tree-lined and very inviting to strollers even on the warmest days of summer. Its saloons and the impressive Ormsby House, where the politicians stayed and dined during the annual legislative sessions, were almost sedate by frontier standards, and no one was allowed inside without a clean shirt and shoes.

Longarm liked Carson City when he wanted to relax and catch up on his sleep. "Megan?"

"Yeah?"

"We could stop here for the night," he said, removing his black Stetson to wipe sweat from his brow. "It's starting to get pretty hot."

"Don't be silly," Megan said. "It's only a little past noon. We've got another seven hours of daylight."

"Just thinking of your horses," Longarm lied. "We don't want to wear them down to a nubbin."

"We won't," she said. "We'll take it slower on down to Topaz Lake at the state line."

Longarm had ridden a stagecoach into Bodie a good many years earlier and, if recollection served him correctly, there was quite a long ways yet to go in order to reach Topaz Lake. It would be a lot more, he thought, than a slow afternoon ride through searing summer heat.

"How much farther is that?"

"Oh," Megan hedged, seeming to read his concern, "we ought to be there by nightfall, if we move along steadily. We can trot more and gallop less."

Longarm didn't like the trot. In fact, he *hated* the trot. He was a good, but not a fine or graceful rider like Megan, and quite frankly, he was a little out of shape for this grueling journey on horseback. Lately Longarm had been traveling overland by train or, when necessity demanded, by stagecoach. Even a buckboard would be preferable at the moment, he figured.

He was still thinking this several hours later as the temperature topped a hundred degrees and they trotted through the sleepy town of Genoa, the oldest settlement in Nevada. Originally founded by the Mormons, it had reluctantly been abandoned by those hardy people when they were called back to Salt Lake City by their leader, Brigham Young. It was no idle fable that said the departing Mormons, made bitter when they were unable to sell their fine and productive farms for more than a few cents on the dollar, had put a curse on Genoa and the surrounding Carson Valley. They'd cursed it with wind, rain, and snow. And sure enough, every time Longarm had ridden through this part of the country a stiff wind was blowing, and just about as often the weather was foul.

"Megan, these horses are starting to get played out," Longarm said.

"Ha! The way I see it, the only one who is getting played out is *you*, Marshal Long."

He grinned sheepishly because it was the truth. The horses, though tired and sweaty, were in superb shape, and Megan looked as fresh as cool apple cider.

It was a very long, very hot, tiring afternoon ride, and by the time they neared the California border, Longarm wasn't grinning about anything. He was saddle-sore and ill-tempered. "There's grass and water here at the lake and this is as far as I'm riding today," he announced in a firm tone of voice.

"All right," Megan said, as agreeably as possible. "We'll camp out here by the side of the lake. My horses hobble well and won't wander. We've got grain for them and food for us. It'll be just fine."

"Glad you agree," Longarm said, only slightly mollified.

"Why don't you gather some driftwood for the fire and I'll lay out things."

"Sounds good."

Longarm wandered over to the edge of the lake. It was big, but not very scenic because most of the surrounding trees had been chopped down by travelers. Topaz Lake was ringed by barren, sagebrush hills, and nestled at the base of the imposing Sierra Nevadas. A late afternoon wind had risen, and it was coming off the mountains cooler and refreshing. The blue surface of the water was marked by whitecaps, and Longarm saw plenty of driftwood for the fire. He began to gather up an armful, and when he had all that he could carry, he trudged on back to their camp.

"That'll do nicely," Megan said. "I'll get a fire going and we'll see if we can get ourselves fed before sundown."

"That would be great," he said, flopping down on his back with a groan of contentment.

"Are you tired or something?" she asked with a half smile.

"Tired? Megan, tired isn't a big enough word for how I feel right now. My butt is on fire and I feel as if I've ridden to hell and back."

"Tsk, tsk," she clucked. "Apparently, you've been spending way too much time in an office chair and not enough in the saddle."

"They don't pay me to ride a horse all over creation," he snapped.

"Then why is it so important that you go down and try to sort things out with Marshal Ivan Kane? I mean, it's not what you are paid to do, is it?"

Longarm sat down cross-legged, facing what was shaping up to be a rather spectacular sunset. "No," he admitted after a moment of deliberation, "it's not what I am paid, as a deputy United States marshal, to do."

"Then, why—"

"Ivan Kane was once a United States federal officer. He was once a federal prisoner. He's been a lot of things, including an inspiration to some of us in the profession.

You see, Megan, he's a man who had to overcome a lot of bad things in his life to become a legend.''

"But now that the legend is crumbling," Megan ventured, "it's ever so important to restore its luster or . . . or else take care of the problem. Is that it?''

"Sort of." Longarm extracted a half-smoked cheroot from his vest pocket. "Kane saved my boss's life once. He saved three other lawmen by busting up an ambush.''

"Oh. So that's it. Your boss owes a debt and he's asking you to repay it for him.''

"I wouldn't put it that way exactly," Longarm said, scowling as he lit his smoke. "I'd just say that Ivan Kane is a man greatly admired by some of us. If he's in trouble, I want to be the one that helps him.''

"But what if, as the telegraph operator said, he's just plain dishonest? That he's been in the job so long that he's tossed out the law books and become a law unto himself?''

Longarm watched as the clouds begin to turn salmon and the sun exploded against the highest Sierra peaks. He smoked for a minute, and then he said, "I'll just have to do whatever is necessary. I can't see into the future.''

"I can," Megan said, starting to prepare their spartan meal of beef and beans. "And I see big trouble.''

"I hope you're wrong.''

"I'm not," she said.

Longarm thought about that all through dinner. Sundown was as brilliant as a bouquet of pink roses. It was nice to sit and watch the sky go through those spectacular changes and then see the first evening stars appear. The heat was swept away in the cool, stiff wind and Longarm, despite his aches and pains, almost felt restored.

"I'm going to take a bath in the lake," Megan said after she'd washed their plates and packed everything

47

neatly away in the saddlebags. "I feel gritty."

"So do I," Longarm said. "Mind if I join you?"

He could not see her face, and therefore her reaction, clearly because of the failed light, but he thought he saw her smile. No matter, because she said, "It's a big lake, Marshal Long. Why don't you find some more of it?"

He didn't have to hide his disappointment. "I guess that means I'll have to wash my own back tonight, huh?"

"I guess it does," Megan said.

"You're a strong woman," Longarm told her. "A real pillar of virtue. Your father sure didn't have anything to worry about, did he."

"Shut up and go for a swim. Don't drown, because then I wouldn't have any excuse to see Bodie, which I've been wanting to do for years."

"It's not so much."

"Neither are you," she said, poking him in the ribs and then hurrying off toward the water.

Longarm couldn't see a lot, only her silhouette, as Megan peeled out of her men's clothes and stood beside the shore. The damned moon was behind the clouds, or he might have gotten a far better view of her lovely body. As it was, he could see just enough to realize that the top half of Miss Megan Riley was every bit as perfect as the bottom half. Her breasts were large, firm, and high. Her waist was very small and her hips, maybe because she spent so much time on horseback, were almost as slender as those of a man.

"Damn," he muttered, smoke trailing dragon-like from his nostrils as he stared at the young, voluptuous woman, who began to walk out into the water.

Longarm stood up and took a half-dozen steps toward Megan, and then he stopped. With a great effort of will he turned east and began to trudge along the lake's shore.

He went about a quarter of a mile before he flopped down on the grass and yanked off his boots. Unbuckling his gunbelt and then undressing quickly, he strode into the cool waters of Topaz Lake. The water burned his saddle sores initially, then it soothed them like a balm. Longarm ducked his head under the surface, and when he raised it, he felt the mountain wind chill his cheeks.

He sighed with pleasure. Despite his physical exhaustion caused by too many unaccustomed hours in the saddle, he went for a long, vigorous swim. The cool, choppy water revived him completely, and when he finally had had enough exercise, he swam back to shore and collapsed naked on the grass, letting the wind dry his body.

"Custis?"

He must have dozed. Starting awake, Longarm sat up. "Yes?"

"Are you all right?"

"I want you, but I also need to sleep."

"Well, come on back to our camp. You can have the sleep at least."

"Yeah," Longarm said, reaching for his things. "I guess a man has to settle for whatever he can get in these parts."

Megan giggled, and then she sashayed off, but not before Longarm realized that she was still naked herself.

Longarm woke up fast, and he hurried to catch up before the girl could get back to their camp.

Chapter 5

Bodie was big, bad, and bawdy despite the fact that the toughest marshal in the West was running things. There had always been a large contingent of fortune seekers who were attracted to Bodie for the same reasons they found the rich mining towns on the Comstock Lode so enticing. Namely, where there was lots of money there was lots of opportunity, and even Ivan Kane's tough reputation did not discourage the boldest of the get-rich-quick types. Bodie had first sprung up in 1859, but it hadn't been until another ten years later that the big strikes had brought nearly ten thousand people rushing to seek their fortune.

"It's not quite as big or busy as it was when I was here two years ago," Longarm decided out loud as they reined up their horses and gazed at the boom town ahead of them. "Do you know what men say when they come here?"

"No."

"Good-bye, God, I'm goin' to Bodie." Longarm smiled. "Of course, that changed some when Ivan Kane arrived in town. "But I well remember that, the first time I came through here, Bodie struck me as just being a maverick. It never seemed to abide by normal standards, and I doubt it even has a church yet, despite the size of its population.''

''But I'll bet it has plenty of saloons.''

''That's a fact.'' Longarm said. ''The town exists mainly because of the Standard Mine and Mill over on Bodie Bluff. It's an exceptionally rich mine, and I think it's safe to say that it's produced millions of dollars worth of ore.''

''Where is it located?''

Just off there to the west. We'll be staying at the U.S Hotel on Main Street, if we get a room.''

''*Two* rooms,'' she said with amusement. ''You never give up, do you.''

''Nope.''

Megan looked right into his eyes and said, ''Good!''

Before Longarm could react, she was moving forward on her sorrel mare and yelling back over her shoulder, ''The first thing we do is find a good stable and take care of these horses. Do you hear me, Marshal Long?''

''Loud and clear,'' he yelled back as he hurried after her.

They attracted a great deal of attention as they rode up Main Street and then turned on King Street and dismounted before the Stuart Kirkwood Livery Stable.

It had a well-run appearance, and Megan went over to a stack of hay and pulled out a handful. She studied it carefully, seemed to approve, and then brought it back to her mare. The horse was so hungry that it gobbled the hay up immediately.

''Their corrals are clean and they feed good alfalfa hay,'' she said. ''I think this will do nicely. How much do they charge a night?''

''I have no idea,'' Longarm said. ''The last time I was

in this town I arrived by stagecoach and left the same way."

"Of course," she told him, a hint of disdain in her voice. "Well, let's find Mr. Kirkwood and make the arrangements."

Kirkwood was out behind the barn working to repair a bridle. When he saw Megan, he smiled broadly. "Howdy, miss! Can I help you in any way a'tall?"

"You can," Megan said. "We've too very good horses that demand the best of care. How much a night?"

"The *best* of care?"

"Within reason," Longarm said. "The United States government won't be gouged."

Kirkwood was a nondescript-looking man in his forties. His face was lined and deeply tanned. He stood up and frowned. "You're with the government?"

"They're paying the feed bill," Longarm said.

"Well then, they can pay it somewheres else," Kirkwood snapped. "Last time some two-bit government official boarded his horse here, I got stuck with a piece of paper that I was supposed to send off somewheres in Denver and I never got any money at all!"

Kirkwood glared at Longarm. "You ain't the fella that did that, are you?"

"How long ago was it?"

"Couple years. Was a big fella, like you. Said he was a marshal. Sort . . . you *are* him!"

"No, I'm not!"

"The hell you say! And you owe me for six nights' board! Be . . . be three dollars and fifty cents interest on my money."

"Go to hell," Longarm growled.

"Pay him," Megan ordered. "Pay the man or you'll not have my horse to ride back to Reno."

"Don't tempt me," Longarm said, digging into his pockets.

When he paid Kirkwood, the liveryman said, "I ain't taking nothin' but cash from you, buddy."

"I ain't your damned buddy."

"Pay him three dollars in advance," Megan said.

"And if I don't, you'll take your horse and ride back to Reno, right?"

"That's right."

"Well, then . . ."

"And you'll never know what might have happened tonight."

"Kee-rist!" Longarm groused, digging back into his pockets and forking over the money. "Megan, you're pushing me to the limit."

"Good."

It took Megan another half hour before she was satisfied that her horses were taken care of well enough to leave. By then, Longarm's gut was growling and he was just about ready to suggest that she find her own accommodations.

"Where is the U.S. Hotel?" she asked.

"Follow me," he said, carrying his saddlebags, rifle, and canteen and letting Megan carry hers.

She followed him up the boardwalk, and the word of her passing swept through the rough saloons so that men set their drinks on the bar and came to admire her as she trudged along. Not a one of them missed the occasion, and it seemed to Longarm that they had to pass every drinking establishment on Main Street. There was the Parole Saloon, the Rifle Club, the Cabinet, the Champion, Mark's Saloon, the Bonanza, and the Sawdust Corner.

"Have you gawky sonsabitches got nothing better to do than to look at a sweet girl from Reno!" he demanded of one particularly rough and leering miner.

"Shut your mouth, cowboy," the miner said. "I'm goin' to make her acquaintance and—"

Longarm didn't let the miner finish. He was a short, powerful sort with a scarred face and a jutting jaw. Longarm snapped the heavy barrel of his Winchester down sharply across the miner's forehead, dropping him like a chopped tree. He stepped over the unconscious man and called back over his shoulder to Megan, "Come along, my dear. We're almost to our room."

Megan muttered something, but Longarm decided it was better that he had not understood. When they finally marched up to the registration desk, Longarm rapped it with his rifle barrel and then he shouted, "Anyone working here?"

A clerk jumped out from behind some curtains. He was a thin, elderly fellow with bat ears and bad eyes. He blinked myopically at Longarm and then he cleared his throat. "It wasn't necessary to bang on our counter or shout, sir!"

"Sorry, but it's been a long day for me and my wife."

Megan inhaled sharply. "Your *what*!"

"My wife, dear. That's you. Remember? How much is your best room?"

"A dollar a night."

"That's outrageous!" Megan cried.

The clerk blinked rapidly. He cleared his throat, drew himself up tall, and pronounced, "You are both more than welcome to find another establishment. There are many to choose from, and I'm sure that you will not mind their lice and bedbugs."

"We'll take a room here," Longarm said.

"Payment in advance, please."

Longarm turned to Megan and looked at her. "Did you

have something else to say, dear?''

Her blue eyes were round. She opened her mouth to speak, then clamped it shut and shook her head back and forth.

"Good," Longarm said. He paid the hotel clerk and entered the name of Thomas Jefferson.

The clerk stared at it for several minutes. He removed his thick spectacles, then stared some more, squinting mightily before replacing his glasses. Finally, he looked up and said, "Are you a descendant of President Jefferson?"

"His great-grandson."

The desk clerk became excited. "My goodness! May I have your autograph!"

"Sure, but it'll cost you a dollar. I get asked so often that my hand is damaged and I have to pay the doctor bills."

"A dollar?" There was a moment of confusion and indecision, then, "Of course!"

Megan pounded Longarm in the spine hard enough to make him grunt with pain. But he got his dollar and room key anyway. They went upstairs, feeling the eyes of several of the patrons boring holes in their backs. Megan wouldn't even look at Longarm when he opened the door and gallantly ushered her inside.

The room was spacious, clean, and beautifully furnished, just like the last room he'd enjoyed here with a certain young lady of the night had been. There were original oil paintings on almost every wall, and although they weren't masterpieces, they were good art. The floors were polished with nice throw rugs, and there were expensive lace curtains on the windows. The furniture was old mahogany, and it glistened with oil. The bedspread was satin with blue swirls on white. A large and ornate chandelier illuminated the room, and there were crystal goblets on a counter in case a guest wished to order wine or even French champagne. And finally, only half hidden by a drape, there was an enormous brass tub with soap and a long-handled scrub brush made of ivory and pure pig-bristles.

"Well," Longarm said, grinning from ear to ear. "Do you still think that this place costs too much?"

"No," she said, tossing her rifle on the bed, then dropping her saddlebags and walking slowly around the room, marveling at the appointments. "It's lovely, really. I'd never have suspected something so fine in a mining town."

"Millionaires want the best," Longarm explained. "And I can assure you that many have stayed here. Most likely, they squandered their quick fortunes and wound up sleeping in the hills, but they had their grand memories."

Longarm went over to the bed and flopped down with a sigh. "How about something to drink, dear?"

"No, thanks," she said, eyeing the bed with growing apprehension.

"Relax," he said. "I'm paying and you can either sleep with me, or I'll give you a blanket and you can sleep on the cold floor."

"Cad."

Longarm shrugged. "Just standing up for my rights. You made me pay that liveryman six dollars, and by damned I'm going to make you responsible for yourself."

"I have been for about the last ten years," she said. "Or didn't you notice that I not only take care of my father, but I break horses and mend saddles and do other leather work."

Longarm relented. "Yes," he said, "you *are* respon-

57

sible and my remark was uncalled for. Megan, you are a very, very responsible girl.''

"I'm a woman. As if you hadn't noticed."

"I have, of course," he said, kicking off his boots and starting to enjoy this banter. "But I just wanted to make sure that *you* remembered that."

"You remind me every time you look at me," Megan said. "And so did those other gawking idiots out on the street. But that still didn't give you the right to crack that one fella's skull."

"Oh, yes, it did," Longarm said, smile melting. "Because the only way you're going to be safe in a place as rough as Bodie is for everyone to know that you're my girl. Period. No doubt about that."

Megan gulped. "I'm packing a pistol."

"Good," Longarm said. "Keep it handy because you will no doubt need it. I can't be watching over you every minute."

Megan sat down on a satin sofa and glanced over at the bathtub. "Do they bring you hot water as part of the room price?"

"Nope. Costs a dollar extra, and there's a tip for the boy who totes the buckets up."

"That's pretty damned high," she said.

"It'll be worth it."

When Megan said nothing else, Longarm added, "Do you see how big the tub is?"

"Of course."

"It's that big so that *two* people can sit inside and bath at the same time. Maybe scrub each other's back."

"And maybe do other things."

"That's right," he said. "Nice things to each other."

Megan took a deep breath and bounced off the sofa. She went to the window and stared out at the street.

"So," she said airily, "this is the famous Bodie."

"It is."

"Maybe we ought to look up Marshal Kane right now."

"Uh-uh," Longarm said, coming up behind her. "I think we need to take a bath together."

Before Megan could respond, Longarm kissed her. For a moment she resisted, but only for a moment. The next thing he knew, she was hugging him tightly and almost cracking his neck. She was kissing him like crazy.

"Easy," he said, pushing her away.

"What's the matter! I thought that you wanted—"

"To take things slow and gentle, Megan. Slow, easy, and gentle. First champagne, then a bath, then the bed. All right?"

"Aren't we even going to eat?"

He laughed outright. "Megan, we can have food sent right up to the room, and that's exactly what we'll do."

"How much money *do* you have?"

"I won three hundred dollars in a poker game the night before I was supposed to board that eastbound train. All of this is coming out of my winnings. Don't worry if spending taxpayers' money is bothering you."

"It is, a little."

"I get an expense account and it's damned spartan. To supplement it, I've learned to play a pretty good hand of poker. That's where the luxuries come from, Megan. That's what makes the difference between enjoying life and just getting along. *Comprende?*"

"Sure," she said.

He went back down stairs and ordered champagne and a bath for two. "Then about nine o'clock, we'll have dinner brought up to us on a silver platter," he told the clerk.

"Of course, Mr. Jefferson," the clerk said, looking extremely impressed. "Anything else?"

"A little brandy. But you can bring that up with the dinner and leave everything to be collected in the morning. I don't want us to be disturbed until then."

"Of course not," the clerk said, bowing slightly. "And may I add that Mrs. Thomas Jefferson is stunning?"

"Of course you may!"

When Longarm went back up to his room, Megan took him by surprise. She was already undressed and in bed with the satin bedcover pulled up to her neck.

"Well now," he said, "I guess if ever a man had to get his balls shot off, having a beautiful virgin like you for the night would be a fair price."

She giggled a little, but it was forced and nervous. "I didn't know if this was the thing to do or if I should wait for the bath."

Longarm unbuckled his gunbelt, and then he went over to the porcelain washbasin and stared at himself in the mirror. "I'm going to shave first just for you, Megan," he told her. "Because once we get started, if I didn't shave I'd probably scratch your face."

Megan gulped. "I know what is going to happen. I've seen a lot of mares bred. I'm a little scared, to be honest."

"Nothing to be scared about," he promised. "Not if we go slow, easy, and gentle."

Megan sighed and closed her eyes. There was a knock at her door, and it startled her so badly that she sat up straight and the bedcover dropped so that Longarm could admire her lovely breasts in good light.

"Come in," he called to the door, his voice already starting to get hoarse with desire. "Megan, better lie back down and cover up."

She flopped back down and lay as still as death. There were two boys and each one had two pails of hot water.

60

When they saw Megan in bed they blushed, but were well enough trained that they didn't stare. In fact, they dumped their water and practically bolted for the hallway, the last one out shouting, "We got two more trips to make in order to fill that tub, Mr. Jefferson!"

"Good," he called.

"Mr. Thomas Jefferson!" Megan exclaimed, shaking her head. "You are *such* a liar."

"Sometimes you have to be," Longarm said, coming over to sit on the bed and kiss her lips.

Megan was already breathing fast. Longarm slipped his hand under the bedcovers and laid it on her warm, muscular thigh. Megan groaned, and Longarm felt himself stiffen. Two more trips he thought, wondering if he could wait so that he did not embarrass those boys anymore.

By the time the tub was filled, Longarm was shaved and the champagne was poured. They each drank, and then they avoided each other's eyes as they quickly climbed into the hot water.

"Oh, dear heavens, this feels wonderful!" Megan squealed, sinking into the suds and closing her eyes.

Longarm slipped his legs around her legs, and then he reached for his champagne glass. "This is going to be a night that neither one of us is ever going to forget, Miss Megan Riley."

"I'm sure that's true for me," she said, eyes popping open, "but I'm also sure that you've done this a thousand times with a thousand different women."

"Wrong."

"Really?"

"Maybe a couple of hundred," he said teasingly, "but probably not a thousand. Although . . ."

She splashed water in his face. "You're awful!"

"No, I'm not," he said, leaning forward and cupping

one of her splendid breasts in his hand and then rubbing its nipple until it grew hard. "And you're going to find that out very, very soon."

"Let's wash up quick and get to it," she breathed. "I've waited too long."

Longarm was of the same strong opinion. They washed, and then they did a lousy job of drying themselves before jumping into the bed. Longarm took her warm, wet body into his arms and began to kiss her sweetly. He was really going to take his time with Megan. He was going to be so slow that she'd moan with desire before he gently entered her and then stirred her passions until she howled with pleasure.

"Hurry," she breathed, legs opening wide. "Put it in now."

"Soon," he promised, fingers slipping down her smooth, wet belly to sink into the mound of her passion.

Megan's back arched and she moaned as his finger gently stroked her most private places. And later, when her heels were raking the silk sheets and Longarm wanted her so bad that his teeth ached and his balls felt as big as balloons, he mounted his Reno virgin. She gasped, and then grabbed his hard buttock and pulled him deeply inside her.

"You feel like a *log* inside of me. A big, hot log!"

"Does it hurt?" he asked anxiously.

"Not anymore," she panted, filling his mouth with her tongue even as her legs began to shake and his body began move over her until they were both lost in a vast, roiling ocean of passion.

Chapter 6

"Are you sure that you want to go along?" Longarm asked. "Marshal Kane can be pretty irascible at times."

"Are you kidding?" Megan asked. "Why would I ever want to miss the chance to meet the legend? Besides, he knows and respects my father. I expect that Marshal Kane will behave like a gentleman."

"I hope so," Longarm said. "But Ivan Kane has always been unpredictable, and that's one of the reasons that he's been able to survive in his profession so long. And frankly, it's also a quality that has caused a lot of people to question his stability."

"Let's go," she said, kissing Longarm on the cheek. "The sooner we meet him and figure out what is the problem, the sooner we can return to our bed and breed some more."

Longarm winced. "We don't call it breeding, Megan."

"But that's what it is," Megan said.

"Yes," Longarm had to agree, "but horses *breed*. People make love."

Megan's eyes twinkled with mischief. "All right, Mr. Know-It-All, what if you just want to breed and you're not the least bit in love?"

63

Longarm pretended shock. "I may have ruined you, Megan. At the very least, I expect that you'll never be quite the same gal again."

"You're right," she said. "And given the way my father acts whenever a man even smiles at me, it's going to be hard to find anyone to replace you, Custis."

"Would he really shoot 'em?" Custis could not forget the solemnity of Wild Bill's grave warning.

"You bet he would," Megan replied. "And tell me this. Is my father the reason why you registered us at the U.S. Hotel as Mr. and Mrs. Thomas Jefferson?"

"Yep. If your father unexpectedly shows up and can't find my name on a hotel register, it might give us time to book separate rooms in another hotel."

"And here I thought you were just being silly."

"Uh-uh," Longarm said. "There'd be nothing silly about it if your father showed up all of a sudden and found us in bed together."

Megan's smile faded and her expression became serious. "Father is going to have to realize sooner or later that I've become a woman. It might as well happen now and with you, Custis."

"Don't say that," Longarm advised. "At least wait until I'm on the train to Denver before you tell him what went on between us here in Bodie."

"All right," Megan promised, taking his arm. "Now let's go meet Ivan Kane."

Longarm headed out the door, and they walked arm and arm down the hallway and the stairs and across the lobby.

"Good morning, Mr. Jefferson, Mrs. Jefferson!" the desk clerk called in cheery greeting.

"Good morning," Longarm responded on his way out.

Marshal Ivan Kane's office was on Main Street, right next to Stillwell's Emporium. As they were walking by the emporium, Megan saw a new and intricately carved saddle in the window which she paused to admire. "Nice workmanship, isn't it?"

"Sure," Longarm said distractedly. "Come on, let's get this meeting over with."

But Megan was leaning up against the window. "There's a saddle shop in there and I can see the man at work."

"Forget about saddles."

But Megan was already heading into the emporium. "You go thaw out Marshal Kane and I'll be along in a few minutes," she called.

Longarm was disgusted, but then he decided that it might be best if he met Ivan Kane in private. After the initial greeting, things could get tense in a big hurry.

Kane's office was small, but as tidy as Longarm remembered. There was one cell in the back of the office, and it was built like a safe with thick strap-iron bars. Kane had an impressive arsenal in his rifle rack, twenty Winchester repeaters and a host of shotguns along with at least half-a-dozen Colt six-shooters. Longarm remembered that Ivan Kane was still one of the finest pistol shots alive, even boasting he could outshoot Wild Bill Hickok.

"Hello, Ivan," Longarm said, opening the door and smiling.

Kane was a tall, powerfully built man. His hair and mustache were silver. He was a fastidious man who had always set himself apart from most frontiersmen by the fact that his clothes were cleaned and pressed, his hair neatly cut, and his boots polished. At first impression, Ivan Kane looked like the town mayor or some other politician. At least he did until you saw the steeliness in his gray eyes. Kane had always been a fooler. He could charm a snake, but then chop off its head quicker than the blink of its eye. When he was in a genial mood, Ivan Kane was witty and good company, but when his mood turned dark, people quickly learned to give him a wide berth.

Kane looked up from the newspaper he was reading and stared at Longarm for a moment before he exclaimed, "Well, damned if it isn't Deputy U.S. Marshal Custis Long!"

"That it is," Longarm said, stepping into the man's office and extending his hand, "and it's good to see you again, Ivan. You're looking as fit as ever."

Kane was proud of his physique as well as his rugged good looks. He stood up, as tall as Longarm and almost as straight. "Why, I never expected to see you back so soon, Custis. Pull up a chair and catch me up on things. How is our little Billy Vail?"

"Fat-assed and happy pushing papers."

Kane chuckled. "Yeah, I imagine that he is. Billy probably cuts a pretty fat hog at the federal office in Denver."

"That he does. He has a clerk who pretty much spoon-feeds him and keeps the office running smoothly. Billy always tells me that he'd like to go back out in the field, but he never will."

"He'd be a fool to," Kane replied, his smile melting. "It's not as easy as it used to be. Things have a way of changing, and not always for the better."

"I know," Longarm said, taking a seat. "Being one of Billy's senior officers, I've been approached about spending more time in administration and even getting a promotion, but I'm not quite ready for that."

"Unless," Kane said, smoothing his mustache with the back of his thumb as was his habit, "you got a good-lookin' gal waitin' for you back in Denver."

They both laughed, but Longarm sensed that Kane was forcing his good humor. Kane cleared his throat and ex-

66

amined his fingernails before he said, "How have you been, Custis?"

"I'm doing just fine."

Kane pinned him with his steel-gray eyes. "So what brings you clear down to Bodie?"

"You never were one to waste time beating around the bush, were you, Ivan."

"Nope. We've always gotten along on good terms, but I know you're not here on a social call."

Longarm had been dreading this moment, and wasn't exactly sure how to begin. He decided to be as direct as Kane and said, "I have a telegram from Denver saying that there's some trouble here in Bodie."

Kane's lips drew back from his teeth. "There's nothing that I can't handle, Custis."

Longarm stood up and walked over to face the window. He stared out in the street for a moment and then said, "I need to be sure of that, Ivan. Those are my orders."

"Goddammit!" Kane shouted, fist smashing down on the top of his desk. "What the hell authority do you—a federal officer—have in my town!"

Longarm turned on his boot heel. "Probably none," he admitted. "But while I may be a federal officer, I'm first and foremost a *lawman*. Just like you, and old Wild Bill Riley, and all the other men who wear a badge and are risking their lives every day to protect the people."

Kane came to his feet, finger stabbing at Longarm. "Don't give me any of your moralistic and high-sounding lectures. You've got *no* authority!"

"We've always worked well together," Longarm said quietly. "We've had a mutual respect that goes back a lot of years. I'm asking you, man to man, to let me stay until I can satisfy Billy Vail that everything is all right here."

Kane came around his desk, face contorted with rage.

"And what if I just kick your ass out of my town and say to hell with friendship! I've told you that everything is fine here in Bodie and that isn't satisfying you. That tells me that you think I'm a liar."

"No," Longarm said, his own voice starting to rise with anger. "It's saying that there may be problems that we can help you with and that—"

"I don't want your goddamn help!" Kane went back to his desk and glared at Longarm. "I want you out of here, Custis. I don't want to fight with you, but I want you out of my town!"

"I'll go," Longarm said, "but if I do, Billy will just send others. So who do you want to deal with, Ivan? Three or four other federal officers, or someone that you can trust and who respects you?"

Kane's cheeks blew out and he swore as he marched back to his cell and kicked it with his boot. "I *hate* it when someone tells me how to do my job. Why, I was a law officer before you were even born!"

"And a good one," Longarm said. "As good as they come."

"And I still am!" Kane shouted, spinning around to glare across his office. "So why can't you and your big-nosed boss just butt the hell out of my business!"

Longarm removed his hat and ran his fingers through his hair. "Pride cometh before a fall, Ivan. There's none of us in this profession that hasn't made some major mistakes. Not one. And sometimes, we need a little help in getting ourselves out of fixes. I'm here to offer that help. It's up to you to be big enough and smart enough to accept that help."

"Shit!" Kane swore. "I been taking care of my own affairs way too damn long to have someone waltz in here and want me to change things around. And I don't know who the hell has been talking 'bout me behind my back, but I mean to find out and see that they never do it again.''

''That would be a big mistake,'' Longarm said. ''People have a right to complain when they think that their officials are doing something wrong.''

''What exactly is the complaint?'' Kane hissed.

Longarm knew that he could not tell this man that there were allegations that he had gone bad. That he was perhaps extorting money from the town merchants and that he had thrown out the law books and become the law of Bodie. That there were men who weren't misfits and outlaws who wanted him either dead, or simply removed from Bodie. That the town was afraid of their marshal and had lost trust in Ivan Kane.

No, Longarm wasn't about to tell his old friend, the legendary Ivan Kane, that people thought that he was corrupt and ruthless.

''The complaint, Ivan, is that you're running a little roughshod over the people and that you're shooting first and asking questions later.''

''Jeezus!'' Ivan shouted, again banging his fist down on his desk. ''Do you know what this town was like when I arrived? Do have any idea what a hellhole Bodie was before the city fathers begged me to clean it up?''

''I know it was wild and woolly.''

''It was a slaughterhouse!'' Kane bellowed. ''Every day men were being gunned down right here on the streets. The city fathers, those chicken-shit sons of bitches, they were so scared of the bad elements that they were paying them off! That's right, bribing them to not to hurt them or their families. And so what happened? The ones with money were safe and everyone else was game for shooting.''

Kane took a deep breath. ''And do you have any idea

how many men tried to tame Bodie before I arrived?''

"No."

"I'll tell you! Better yet, I'll take you up to Boot Hill and I'll show you their graves." Kane smiled wickedly. "You see, they laid them out side by side. "Nine marshals shot between 1870 and 1880—almost one a year. In fact there'd have been a lot more than that, but most of the time they didn't even have a marshal because no one would take the job at any price!''

"Why?"

Kane blinked. "What do you mean, why?"

"Why was Bodie so much worse than any other boom town with all its wild elements?''

Kane took a deep breath. "Bodie, from the beginning, was founded by corrupt men. They got here first and they set up things exactly as they wanted. They made the law and then they eliminated anyone who tried to change their rules.''

"So who hired the lawmen who were gunned down?''

Kane opened a desk drawer and drew out a silver flask. He waved it in Longarm's direction, but the offer was declined so Kane continued speaking.

"After a few years, some honest merchants came into Bodie. There was a newspaper editor, a fella named Joe Barnes. He wrote editorials inciting the good citizens to band together and form vigilante committees, if necessary, to reclaim Bodie.''

"And did they?"

"They tried a few times, but their leaders, including Joe Barnes, were always shot down. Sometimes from ambush and sometimes right out in front of everyone in the street, sort of as a lesson.''

"And this just went on and on?"

"That's right." Kane's eyes squinted. "The year before I came, two federal officers like you came through Bodie nosin' around, and they both vanished.''

"Vanished?" Longarm hadn't heard of this.

"That's right," Kane said, "vanished. Their bodies were later discovered at the bottom of a couple of mine shafts. No bullet wounds. They were sent over from the district office in San Francisco.''

"I see," Longarm said, knowing that this was a plausible explanation and that it was commonplace for one district office not to have any idea what another was or was not doing.

"Anyway," Kane said, "I walked into this hornet's nest knowing its bloody history. I brought along two deputies from the last town where I'd been working. Both were ambushed and are buried in Boot Hill. Neither one lasted more than three months. So I started getting just as tough as the men that were trying to plant me up there with the others.''

"What did you do?"

"I got a judge to come through every month and I . . . I convinced him that he needed to be the hanging judge of Nevada. He started meting out justice rope-style.''

"You mean he began to rubber-stamp executions.''

"No, dammit! He started to get some backbone and was doing real well.''

"Until?"

"He was gunned down too." Kane took another drink. "So what was I to do then? I couldn't get another judge to even consider coming through Bodie. It was akin to setting their own death sentence.''

"So *you* became the judge.''

"That's right!" Kane exclaimed, waving his flask in the air. "I just said to myself that I had only two choices, either arrest those that would come peaceably and then sentence them, or else gun them down and be done with them just like a man would do when he finds a rattlesnake in his backyard.''

"How many rattlesnakes have you killed so far?'' Longarm asked quietly.

"Huh?''

"You heard me. How many?''

Kane stood up, eyes shining with pride. "I guess I've had to exterminate about twenty men so far—but that's over the years, you understand.''

"And how many rattlesnakes do you suppose are still out there waiting to creep into your yard?''

Kane chuckled. "You're trying to box me into something here, aren't you, Custis. You're trying to get me to stick my head through a noose.''

"No, I'm not,'' Longarm said. "But I need to know what the future is going to hold. And then we need to decide what we ought to do next.''

"You don't need to do anything except to get out of my town.''

"It's not *your town*,'' Longarm said tightly. "Nobody owns a town, they just own some property. That's all.''

"There are men here who think differently and are willing to kill to prove it,'' Kane said. "I have to deal with them before they deal with me and . . .''

Whatever else Kane was about to say was forgotten as Megan Riley stepped into his office.

She smiled, then turned to address Longarm. "Everything all right, Custis?''

"Yeah,'' he replied, studying Kane's face. "This is just a friendly meeting among old friends, right, Ivan?''

"That's right,'' Ivan said, slipping his flask back into his desk drawer. "And who is this beautiful girl, Custis?

Here we were jawin' about this and that, and you've been keeping her all to yourself.''

"Miss Megan Riley, I want you to meet Marshal Ivan Kane.''

"I've heard so much about you from my father,'' Megan said, coming across the room with her hand extended. "It's an honor, Marshal Kane.''

Kane beamed. "So, you're Old Wild Billy Riley's pride and joy!''

"I wouldn't go that far,'' Megan said. "But I am his only child and his best friend.''

"How is he?''

"His eyes and his health aren't what they used to be,'' Megan said bluntly. "But he still gets around and can be pretty cantankerous. In fact, he's still awful randy.''

Kane barked a laugh and the pair shook hands. "You're just as frank as your father, but a whole lot prettier. Where are you staying, Miss Riley?''

"The U.S. Hotel.''

"I'd like to escort you to dinner one of these nights, if you're going to be staying in my town.''

Megan glanced over at Longarm. "I haven't heard yet. Custis, are we staying in Bodie?''

Custis looked to Kane. "Yeah, unless the marshal has some objection?''

"Hell, stay as long as you want!'' Kane exclaimed. "But you need to be careful, Miss Riley. I'll probably have to escort you about. I do my damnedest, but there's still some bad men in this town and a pretty young woman like you can't be too well protected.''

Megan, however, went over to Longarm and slipped her arm through his. "Custis is my protection, Marshal Kane. But I wouldn't mind a little extra help, and I'm sure that Custis wouldn't mind it either. Would you, darling?''

Longarm blushed. The little schemer was sewing him and Kane up together tighter than two weasels in a feed bag. "No," he said tightly. "I wouldn't mind at all."

"Fair enough, then," Kane said, reaching for his hat. "Why don't I give you both a little walking tour of my town?"

"All right," Megan said brightly, "that would be fun."

"And maybe exciting too," Kane said, with a wink of his eye.

Chapter 7

"Walk just slightly behind me," Kane said to Longarm as they exited his office, "and keep your hand near your gun butt and your eyes moving."

"Kee-rist!" Longarm swore. "If you're that worried, then we've no business bringing Megan along."

"I'm not worried as long as she stays behind us," Kane said. "And while I don't expect any trouble, you know as well as I do that a man can never be too damned careful."

Longarm started to insist that Megan return to their hotel, but the girl must have read his mind because she shook her head. "I've heard so much about Bodie I'm not about to miss the chance to see it up close."

To say that Longarm felt on edge as they started down the boardwalk of Main Street would have been a gross understatement. They passed the Mono Brewery and Saloon, where Kane ducked his head inside and studied the patrons with an especially hard look before continuing along.

"Trouble there?" Longarm asked.

"Always," Kane said. "I don't like the owner and he

doesn't like me. He gets to talking behind my back and some of his drunks will come hunting me. I've had to crack down pretty hard on 'em a time or two.''

As they continued along, a well-dressed man stepped out of the Can Restaurant and started to walk past, but Kane grabbed his sleeve.

''Mr. Johnson! Why, didn't I tell you to get out of town last week?''

The man tried to bat Kane's hand away, but the marshal grabbed the front of his jacket and pulled his face close. Longarm stiffened when Kane hissed, ''I know you were trying to get someone to take a shot at my back.''

''No, sir, Marshal!'' the man cried. ''You got it all wrong!''

In answer, Kane slammed the man up against the wall and grabbed his throat. ''I'll give you just one hour to get your lying ass out of my town. One hour!''

Longarm started to intercede, but Megan blocked his path and shook her head no. Longarm watched as Kane banged Johnson's head up against the wall so hard that the man's eyes crossed.

''Now git!'' Kane shouted. ''You're just damned lucky we're in the company of a lady or I'd smear your lying face all over the wall.''

Johnson swayed off down the street. When he started to turn into a small office building where the sign THAD-DEUS BLAKE, PHYSICIAN AND SURGEON hung over the walk, Kane bellowed, ''You better not stop in my town! Go on!''

The dazed man glanced over his shoulder, and Longarm saw the terror as well as the confusion. Then the man staggered on down the street.

Kane wasn't paying Johnson any more attention. He was glaring at the spectators who had suddenly appeared, and now he shouted, "All of you, get back to your business! Haven't any of you gawky bastards got anything worthwhile to do!"

Longarm watched as the sullen townspeople turned away and went back into their shops and saloons. He caught Megan's eye, and he could see shock and concern. Longarm considered having a word with Marshal Kane, but decided this was probably neither the time nor the place.

Kane moved on. As they passed a small group of miners, the men's conversation fell off and they got interested in their hands and feet, refusing to look up or even acknowledge Kane.

"As you can see," Kane said drily, "people are not real friendly in Bodie. These men, for example, probably drank and whored away all their wages and are just trying to decide how they can recoup their losses."

One of the miners looked up suddenly and his eyes were venomous. "Marshal Kane, we ain't pissed away anything. We're just here havin' a little conversation and a few beers until it's time to go back to work at the mines."

"You sayin' I'm wrong?" Kane asked, his voice dropping to barely a whisper. "Your name is Clyde Harding, isn't it?"

"Yeah, but—"

"And aren't you the fella that I had to put in jail about . . . oh, three weeks ago for being drunk and disorderly?"

"That's right," Harding choked. "And you opened my skull up with the barrel of that hog-leg on your hip."

"I guess that some men take a little more teaching than others," Kane said, eyes boring into the group. "So why don't you men just start on back to work right dammed now? That way, you'll be completely sober by the time you reach the mines and you won't make mistakes and get yourselves or anyone else killed or hurt.''

Harding stood up. He was a big man, but stooped from too many years of brutal, backbreaking work in the mines. ''You'd think, Marshal, that the merchants here in town wouldn't be too happy about you runnin' off their cash-payin' customers.''

Kane's mouth drew down into a hard line. ''Start walking while you still can.''

The men walked. Kane stared after them, and when he became aware that Megan and Longarm were staring at him, he swung about and said, ''That Harding is a mean-tempered sonofabitch. He comes on real nice when he's sober, but when he's drinking, he gets vicious. He'd already messed up the faces of two of his drinking buddies when I arrested him. He swore he'd kill me some day.''

''He's a miner,'' Longarm said.

''He's a snake that can bite you from behind and kill you as dead as anything,'' Kane countered.

They continued on up the street and were passing BOONE & WRIGHT—GENERAL MERCHANDISE when a middle-aged man with muttonchop whiskers hailed them.

''Marshal Kane!''

Ivan whirled, hand dropping to the butt of his six-gun. Longarm grabbed Megan, shielding her body.

''Marshal Kane?''

''Relax,'' the marshal said to Megan and Longarm. ''It's a friend.''

''I'm glad to hear that you have one in Bodie,'' Megan said icily.

''I've got a lot of friends in this town,'' Kane replied. ''They just don't make a big show of it, that's all.''

78

Longarm watched as the marshal walked over to have a few words in private with the man who had hailed him. He could not hear the conversation, but there seemed to be some sort of disagreement and probably fearing their words would be overheard, the pair stepped into a side alley.

"I've never seen anything like this," Megan whispered to Longarm. "This town is about ready to explode."

"I know," he said. "I'm surprised that Kane is still alive. Megan, you can almost *feel* the hatred these people have for him."

"My father was tough," Megan said, "but he was a pussycat compared to Ivan Kane. Why do they keep him in office?"

Longarm glanced back at the side alley. "That's a good question and one that I'll have to get to the bottom of before I leave."

"Shh!" Megan whispered. "Here he comes!"

Kane was smiling when he reappeared, but the man he had spoken to looked anything but happy as he went back inside his emporium.

"Custis. Megan. I apologize for not making the proper introductions, but that was Mr. Harvey Boone, who, along with J.W. Wright, owns this thriving establishment."

"Mr. Boone appeared to be very upset about something," Longarm said.

"Oh, he was!" Kane chuckled. "He had just gotten wind that it was time for my annual raise. And since Mr. Boone and Mr. Wright are among the most prosperous of our merchants and proprietors, they will have to pay accordingly."

"Your wages are not paid by taxes?"

"What taxes?" Kane snickered. "The last time that Mono County tried to assess a business or sales tax, the

79

tax collector was beat to a pulp and run out of town on a rail!"

"Did you arrest those responsible?" Longarm asked.

"Those responsible wore masks and the attack took place in a whorehouse about midnight. No, Kane said, looking amused, "I think you can well imagine that the tax collector was not very popular and there were no witnesses to the beating."

"I see."

"Good," Kane said, "because it's important that you do see."

"How much is your salary?" Megan blurted out.

Kane had been about to continue their walk down the boardwalk, but now he suddenly stopped, planted his feet, and said, "I'm not sure that is any of your business, young lady."

"My father was the marshal of Reno for sixteen years and never made more than a hundred dollars a month."

"Well, pity him," Kane snapped. "Maybe he should have come to a town like Bodie where everyone was trying to kill him so that they could return to their lawless and wicked ways."

"My father," Megan said defiantly, "had plenty of troubles in Reno, and he was shot three times in the line of duty, but he always came back and made sure that the law was upheld. And by that, I mean the laws of the State of Nevada."

"Well," Kane said, voice taking on a hard edge, "this is California, and it's a boom town with all that trash and riffraff that big money attracts. We have no civic committees. There are no church socials along the Truckee riverside, and you'd be damned hard pressed to find anyone who owns a bible."

Kane started walking, leaving Longarm and Megan to

either hurry after the man or to give up the excursion. They hurried after Kane, who shouted over his shoulder, "Miss Riley, your father had a bunch of Sunday-school kids compared to what I have to deal with every day here in Bodie. He has no idea what tough really is, Miss Riley. I know he thinks that he's had some close shaves and been in some tight fixes, but he hasn't. Not really."

"You're an arrogant ass!" Megan shouted. "You dare to say that my father had it easy!"

"Compared to what I've had to fight in my town, yes."

"That ties it," Megan said, eyes blazing. "I'm going back to the hotel."

"I'd better escort you," Longarm said.

"We'd *both* better escort her," Kane stated flatly. "The few respectable women in Bodie are known to most everyone. All the others are just assumed to be whores. And you, miss, dressed in those man's clothes but showing all the curves of a young woman, would prove to be a riddle that the more unsavory element in Bodie would find irresistible."

"I can take care of myself," she said.

Kane looked at Longarm. "I think you had better get her attention, Marshal Long. This is no time for a female temper tantrum. This young lady needs to be educated about life in a mining camp."

"He's right," Longarm said. "You can't just stomp off and expect that, because you pack a six-gun or a derringer, you're going to be all right. It doesn't work that way in a town like this."

"Why not!" Megan swung around and looked up and down the street. "This place strikes me as being *evil*!"

"That's because it is," Kane said, offering her his arm, which Megan ignored.

"If it's so evil, why haven't you done something to change it?"

Kane shrugged, his craggy face hardening. "The only thing that can shackle the greed and evil in evil men is fear. If they fear punishment, they will desist from acts of wrongdoing."

He turned to Longarm. "You've been in more than a few towns like this, Custis. Why don't you tell this young lady the truth? Am I right, or am I wrong?"

"You're right," Longarm said. Then he added, "But there are a lot of men who are neither good nor evil, but something in the middle. In fact, I think that most men fall into that category. And those people can often be appealed to in a decent, understanding manner. They respond to reason, not the constant threat of fear."

"That's bullshit!" Kane removed his pocket watch and said, "I need to continue on my rounds, and Custis, you need to take this innocent young lady back to her room. Therefore, I think this is the end of our little tour of Bodie. It probably wasn't a very good idea anyway."

Longarm saw Megan's cheeks flame with anger, but he took her arm and, while leading her away, called back, "I'll be talking to you soon, Marshal."

"Do yourselves a big favor and buy a stage ticket back to Reno!"

"We came here on horses!" Megan screeched.

"Then saddle them up and ride," Kane yelled as he marched on down Main Street, hand shading the butt of his gun, eyes constantly shifting.

"What are we going to do!" Megan whispered, her voice filled with fury and anguish. "That man is terrible."

"He didn't used to be that way."

"But he is now!"

"I think I'm going to have to get some evidence against

him and then see that he is removed."

"By whom! You're a federal officer and he's a local constable."

"There is a federally chartered bank here in Bodie. A federal post office too. And Wells Fargo and Company operates out of here and they have federal contracts," Longarm said. "Billy Vail knows that and he'll expect me to use it all to put my foot down hard and straighten this mess out."

"I don't think you can," Megan said.

"I'm not afraid of Ivan Kane."

"You should be," Megan said. "And if you think that he is operating this . . . this fiefdom on his own, you are wearing blinders."

"What's that supposed to mean?"

"It means that, as sure as the sun will come up tomorrow morning, Ivan Kane has people that hold even *him* accountable. Men who use him to retain their power and influence."

"You sound pretty sure of that."

"I am sure! Kane has the gun, but even if they're paying him two hundred dollars a month, that's nothing compared to the money that is supposed to be coming out of these mines. And I can tell you something else."

"I'm not sure that it's something I want to hear."

"You're going to have to hear it anyway," Megan said. "This town is not only evil, it's rotten to the core. I will bet you anything that there are things going on here that will put Ivan Kane behind bars for the rest of his natural life."

"I hope you're wrong, Megan. He's a legend."

"He's a tyrant! A killer with a badge."

Longarm took Megan's arm and escorted her back toward the hotel. As they were about to pass a man, he stepped in front of Longarm and, after looking up and down the street, said, "My name is Henry Olliver. Stuart Kirkwood said you're a federal marshal."

"I am."

"A friend of Marshal Kane?"

"An acquaintance," Longarm said cautiously. "Why do you ask?"

"We desperately need help."

"You want to talk about it in private?"

"Yes!" The man was practically quaking in his shoes.

"All right," Longarm said. "We'll meet tonight. Where is best for you?"

"North end of town outside of Harkin Livery. Ten o'clock. And don't let Marshal Kane follow you!"

"I won't," Longarm said tightly.

The man hurried away.

"See," Megan said as they went back to their hotel. "I told you things were rotten in Bodie."

Chapter 8

Longarm climbed out of bed and looked down at Megan. "I think we'd better rest for a while."

She stretched and ran her hands down across her flat belly and then her muscular thighs. Just looking at her made Longarm begin to ache again with passion, but he knew that he had to start getting ready for his meeting with Henry Olliver.

"I'll be waiting up for you," Megan said with a slow smile. "Don't be too long, Custis."

"Get some sleep."

"Sleep, my darling, is not what I hunger for right now."

"I'm beginning to think you're insatiable."

"I certainly hope so."

Longarm chuckled and pulled on his pants, then his socks, and finally his boots. He grew serious thinking about the meeting that was about to take place. "Megan, I have a terrible feeling that I'm going to get some evidence against Ivan Kane that could send the man to prison."

"That may well be the case," Megan said. "But you're

not the judge and the jury like Kane appears to be in Bodie. All you can do, Custis, is conduct your investigation and gather up whatever evidence you can, and then decide whether you need to arrest him or not.''

"You make it sound pretty cut and dried.''

"It is, really. But instead you're doing what my father always said a lawman can't afford to do.''

"And that is?''

"Let his personal feelings affect his decisions.''

Longarm reached for his shirt. "Well, it's damned hard not to. You see, I think a person's life is sort of like a balancing scale. By that I mean that we all do things we're not very proud of and would like to erase. But most of us also do some fine things that we are proud of, and we need to balance everything out.''

"That's certainly an interesting philosophy for a lawman,'' Megan said. "Are you trying to tell me that, if a man is good to his wife, children, and friends, yet robs a bank or store, his sentence ought to account for his good deeds? That he ought to be shown leniency?''

"Judges weigh a man's background into their sentencing. If someone has been a pillar in the community and it is a first-time offense, he'll get a far lighter sentence than a career outlaw. So yes, I think that there is a balancing of the good along with the bad.''

"And you think that maybe Ivan Kane, because of all the good things he has done, ought to be given some extra consideration even if he is abusing his office?''

"Yes.''

"I strongly disagree,'' Megan said. "Someone like Ivan Kane gives a black eye to every decent man who ever wore a badge. If he really is guilty and that is proven in a court of law, people all over Nevada will say, 'See, another lawman gone bad. They're probably all bad and it's just Ivan Kane that got caught.' "

"Well," Longarm said, cinching on his gunbelt. "We're talking as if Kane has already been tried and convicted. And of what? We don't have any evidence of wrongdoing."

"You don't think what he did to that man whose head he smashed into the storefront was wrong?"

"I think it was too harsh," Longarm admitted, "but we don't know what Mr. Johnson really did or is. And Ivan may be right, the man might actually be behind an attempt on his life."

"You're bending over way too far in Kane's favor," Megan said. "And I know that, if you have to arrest him, it's going to be very, very difficult for you, Custis. You just need to start thinking about how best you can do your job and not about the consequences."

"You sound like a judge or something," Longarm said, feeling a little irritated.

"My father is a lawman, and his personal feelings for someone never interfered with his good judgment. And I can tell you that, although he seems loud and insensitive, there were a few times when he cried alone because he had to arrest someone that he either called a friend or had admired. You've got to do the same with Ivan Kane, if that's what it takes."

Longarm picked up his Stetson and jammed it down on his head hard. He didn't like to hear what Megan was saying, but he knew that she was right.

"I'll be back before midnight," he told her.

"A kiss good-bye?"

"Sure," he said, marching over to the bed.

He'd meant to kiss her quickly and then be gone, but Megan pulled him down on top of her. She squirmed and thrust her chest out, and damned if he could resist. Taking

87

a soft breast into his mouth, he laved her nipples with his tongue until she began to moan with pleasure.

"Come back to bed, just for a minute," Megan pleaded.

"I can't," he said. "It's almost ten and I just got dressed."

"You don't even have to undress," she breathed. "You don't even have to take off your boots or your hat. Just your gunbelt and undo a few buttons. What do you say?"

"What have I gotten into," Longarm panted as he unbuckled his gunbelt and let it slip to the floor. He threw his hat aside and unbuttoned his pants. A moment later, he was driving in and out of Megan, the toes of his boots digging into the sheets and generally making a mess of them.

"Oh," she gasped, her body thrusting powerfully, her hands slipping into his back pockets and jerking his buttocks up and down, "you are my *stallion*!"

Longarm didn't argue the fact. In truth, he could not get enough of this filly, and if he hadn't been committed to duty, he would have just said to hell with Henry Olliver and kept screwing Megan until they both wore themselves down to a nubbin.

But thirty minutes later, he was standing a little weak-kneed and shaky in the shadows near the Harkin Livery.

"Dammit, Henry," Longarm muttered after a quarter hour of waiting had passed. "I gave up a hell of a lot to be here on time, Now where the hell are you!"

Longarm waited another fifteen minutes and, when Olliver still didn't show, said to hell with it and started back to his hotel room, the musky sex-scent of loving Megan thick in his nostrils. He was halfway across the street when he saw someone coming up the boardwalk.

Someone moving very cautiously and trying to stay in the shadows.

"Olliver?" Longarm hissed, cupping his hands to his mouth. "Is that you?"

"Yes! Shhhh!"

Longarm frowned, thinking that this was sure a rabbity kind of fellow, and . . .

Three shots rang out from across the street. Longarm could see Henry Olliver's silhouette. The silhouette began to run in panic.

Longarm jumped forward and a bullet grazed his temple. He lost his balance for an instant and struck the ground. He tried to yell to Olliver to get down and take cover, but two more shots shattered the night air and Henry Olliver, running full bore up the street, lifted onto his toes.

Longarm, trying to shake his vision back into place and track the location of the muzzle flashes, blinked, and then saw Olliver dance forward a few steps before collapsing in a heap.

"Sonofabitch!" Longarm wailed, rolling in behind a water trough and struggling to gather his wits. "Sonofabitch!"

Two more shots followed in quick succession, and both of them had Longarm's name. Fortunately, the water trough was made of heavy, water-soaked planking and proved to be an effective shield.

Longarm touched his temple, and his fingers were smeared with blood. He reached for his bandanna, and then he reached up and dunked it into the trough. The cold water felt good and it revived his senses.

Who was trying to kill him? Marshal Ivan Kane? That was a strong possibility.

Longarm waited a couple of moments. He halfway expected citizens to come out to investigate the scattered gunfire, and then he would feel more comfortable standing up in full view. But no one came to investigate until Marshal Kane himself arrived.

"You!" Kane shouted, gun out and pointed at the water trough. "Throw your gun out and stand up or I'll blast you to pieces!"

"Marshal, it's me! Custis Long!"

"Custis?" The gun dropped a fraction.

"Yeah."

"What the hell are you doing out here by yourself on the street at this time of night? Someone shot Henry Olliver down. Were they trying to rob you men?"

Longarm climbed off his belly. He dunked his throbbing head in the water trough and then replaced his hat. It was more of a struggle than he'd expected just to gain his feet.

"Jezus, Custis! Have you been shot too?"

Kane holstered his gun and jumped over to offer support, but Longarm pushed him off. "I'm just grazed. What about Olliver?"

"He died up the street. He was gone before I could even get to him," Kane said, shaking his head.

Longarm hurled his sopping handkerchief away and stepped back, his gun still in his right hand. "Ivan, I want to see your pistol."

"What?"

"Your pistol!" Longarm's command was harsh. "Goddammit! Hand it over."

But Kane retreated, shaking his head. "You think . . . you think that *I* shot you and Henry Olliver?"

"I don't know what to think!" Longarm raged. "But I want to see your pistol. If it's got six beans and hasn't been fired, then I'll have my answer."

"Dammit, I just fired it! I saw the muzzle flashes of the gun that killed Oliver and grazed you. I fired three rounds at the man, but missed and he got away."

For one of the first times in his life, Longarm was seized with indecision. Ivan Kane might well be telling the truth.

"I'm not handing my gun over to you," Kane vowed, hand shading his gun. "You're going to have to take it from my dead body, Custis. Because I'm still the law in this town and you are the one that is going to have to answer some questions about this shooting."

Longarm knew that he was trapped. There was no way that he would kill Marshal Kane under these circumstances. As of yet, he had no evidence of any wrongdoing on the marshal's part, and since Kane's gun was in his holster and Longarm's gun was in his fist, it would be tantamount to murder.

"All right," he said bitterly as he jammed his six-gun back into his holster. "What the hell do you want to know?"

"What were you doing out here in the dark at this hour?"

"I was supposed to meet Henry Olliver."

"Why?"

"He wanted to talk to me in private."

"About what?" Kane said, body poised like a steel coil.

"I don't know."

"You're lying!"

Longarm stiffened and said, "If you weren't a lawman, I might be inclined to kill you for saying that, Ivan. But I'm going to let it pass this time. I told you the truth. Olliver knew I was a U.S. marshal. He sounded like he was in a bad fix and he wanted to talk to me in private.

That's as much as I can tell you."

"He should have come to me, damn his eyes!" Kane kicked the water trough so hard it spilled over. "He should have come to *me*!"

"Maybe so," Longarm said. "But he didn't."

"And it cost the fool his life."

Longarm took a deep breath. His head was beginning to throb like a Kiowa drum.

"I'm going back to my room and get some rest," he told Kane. "That is, if you have no more questions."

"I do have more questions," Kane snapped angrily. "But they can wait until morning. Be at my office by nine o'clock."

Longarm didn't say another word as he shuffled back up the street toward the U.S. Hotel. He felt dazed, weak, and thoroughly confused by this tragic turn of events. When he came to Henry Olliver's body, he knelt beside the corpse and saw that the man had been shot twice, both times in the back. Olliver had skidded on his belly across the dirt, and now he lay with bulging eyes staring into the dirt.

"I'm sorry I couldn't help you," Longarm muttered before he plodded on toward the hotel and the comfort of Megan Riley's arms.

Chapter 9

Longarm dragged himself out of bed the next morning and staggered over to the mirror. "I look like I've been pulled sideways through a knothole, Megan."

"Getting shot and making love all night will do that to a man when he gets a little age on him," Megan said, looking devilishly happy for such an early hour. "Are you going to take me to breakfast before you go see Marshal Kane?"

"Sure," Longarm said. "After last night, this poor old body could definitely use some replenishing."

"It won't take me long," Megan said, jumping out of bed and grabbing her pants.

Longarm, despite his aches and pains, had to grin. Megan was a like a schoolgirl, and Longarm knew that he was her first real beau. Flushed from a night of lovemaking and filled with innocence and wonder at the pleasure that a man and a woman could bring each other, Megan was a joy to watch.

"I hope you have some money," she said, "because I'm famished. I want a steak, some fried potatoes, eggs, and lots of coffee and maybe even a slice of pie for dessert."

"You're going to be expensive to keep if you eat every meal like that," he said as he slowly dressed. "And what are you going to do while I'm trying to get to the bottom of Bodie's can of worms?"

"I'm going to go to Stuart Kirkwood's and look at some horses and saddles," she informed him. "Maybe I can find some bargains to buy and then resell in Reno."

"You're a horse trader, huh?"

"I generally do pretty well," Megan said, hitching up her pants and buckling her belt around her narrow waist. "You see, at first men tend to think of me as helpless and naive. Then, after I begin to dicker with them on a horse or piece of tack, they often get mad and think I've no business knowing as much as I do about horses and saddles. They'll generally try to dazzle me with their knowledge, and so I just listen and nod my head."

"And play dumb?"

"For a while," Megan said. "For as long as I can stand it while they blow off steam. Sooner or later, though, I just get fed up with their bullshit and lay things on the line. I tell 'em everything that is wrong with their horses and saddles. That really puts their noses out of joint."

"Hell of a way to get on their good side," Longarm said dryly.

"Well," Megan said, "I'm not finished. You see, after I sort of pick their property apart, then I say something nice about the horse or the saddle. That throws them off balance, and that's when I hit 'em with an offer."

"A damned *low* offer, I'll bet."

"Yes, but they'll almost always take it and then tell their friends how they slickered a damned woman."

"And do they sometimes?"

Megan shrugged. "I've never bought a lame horse that some crook has managed to sneak by me as sound. And

I've bought quite a few that were thought to be hopeless cases either because of unsoundness or bad habits that made them very undesirable or even dangerous.''

"And I suppose you have your 'special' ways of breaking and training outlaws?''

"Of course,'' Megan said, unable to mask her pride. "Basically, I spend more time with problem horses than anyone else has been willing to devote. If the animal has leg problems, I wrap the tendons and joints and use balms and even blisters. If the animal has bad feet, I keep them clean and medicated. If he has worms or has been foundered or—''

"I get the idea,'' Longarm said, cutting her off. "And I suppose, if we're talking saddles, you just replace the worn or rotten leather and redo the stitching, that sort of thing.''

"Exactly.'' Megan pulled on her shirt and buttoned it to the neck. "You wouldn't believe some of the old saddles that I've restored to better than new.''

"Yes, I would,'' Longarm said, touching the wound at his temple to make sure that Megan's bandage was still in place. "Are you ready to go?''

"Almost,'' she said, reaching for her boots.

Their breakfast together was uneventful other than the fact that they both ate as if they were winter-starved wolves.

"Just keep bringing the food,'' Longarm told the cafe owner. "We'll keep eating and paying for it until we're full.''

"Yes, sir,'' the man said, shaking his head and wiping his hands on his apron. He looked at Megan and said, "No offense, miss, but I sure do admire a woman with a hearty appetite who manages not to get as big as a cow.''

Megan, mouth full of ham and eggs, nodded.

When they left the cafe, Longarm consulted his pocket watch. "It's five minutes after nine. I'd better get to moving over to Kane's office before he comes gunning for me."

"Are you serious?"

"No," Longarm said.

"Then don't joke about something like that. It makes me very nervous."

"I apologize." Longarm took Megan in his arms and gave her a kiss right out in front of everyone. Then he pointed her in the direction of the Kirkwood livery and went to meet Marshal Kane.

Kane was waiting for him with more coffee. The marshal of Bodie took one look at Longarm and said, "You look used up, Custis. What's the matter, is that Riley girl a little too much for you all night?"

Longarm decided to ignore the remark. He took his coffee and then took a seat. There was another man in the office and he was wearing a badge.

"This is Deputy Hec Ward," Kane said by way of introduction. "He's worked on and off for me about two years. He's a good man with a gun."

Longarm put the cup of hot coffee to his lips and studied Ward. The man was in his early twenties, and his most obvious feature was that he was missing his left arm below the elbow. Ward had gotten a blacksmith to make him a hook that was long, curved, and sharp-pointed. The man was big and wore a full and completely unruly black beard. There was nothing friendly-looking about him. He looked, quite honestly, like a French pirate or buccaneer.

"Howdy," Longarm said over his coffee cup.

Ward barely nodded his head in greeting. He scratched his belly with the point of his hook and glared at Longarm with the dark, merciless eyes of an eagle.

96

"Hec Ward is the only man in Bodie right now that I know can stand up to the harassment and threats that come with wearing a badge in this town," Kane said. "We've been through some scrapes before."

"Yeah," Longarm said, eyeing the man. "It looks like you have."

Kane's eyebrows lifted. "Are you referring to his missing hand and lower arm?"

"Maybe."

"Hec, why don't you tell the marshal how you lost 'em."

Ward's eyebrows were as thick and bushy as black caterpillars, and he clearly did not want to explain anything to Longarm. But under Ivan Kane's steady and unyielding gaze, he cleared his throat and said in a deep voice, "I lost 'em in a mine explosion up on the Comstock Lode. Some sonofabitch messed up the charge and I was the only one that was willin' to try and fix it."

"And that's what you got for your trouble," Longarm said. "That's a shame."

"I don't mind so much. The hook works good and nobody wants to mess with me."

"I'd guess not."

"I hear you're real good with that six-gun, Long."

"I'm not bad."

"I'm pretty good myself. Maybe we'll go out to the edge of town sometime and shoot targets for two bits a pop."

"Maybe."

Kane let the two men take each other's measure for a few more minutes, and then he came over and sat beside Longarm. He kicked his polished boots up on his desk, leaned back, and laced his fingers behind the back of his head before saying, "Tell me again exactly what happened last night."

"All right." Longarm repeated the account and changed nothing. He had heard so much testimony and denial by accused men that, like most lawmen, he had become an expert in catching people in their inconsistencies. There were none in his story about Henry Olliver.

"So," Longarm ended up saying, "that's the way it was. Now, I'd like to know what had Olliver terrified and who are your murder suspects."

"Hec and I think that Olliver was gunned down by a consortium of saloon owners," Kane said. "You see, there has always been a power struggle among them in this town. Another faction, the mine owners and the miners' union, has also resorted to violence in order to achieve their aims."

"And you haven't been able to make a peace between them?" Longarm asked.

"I've tried," Kane said, a touch of bitterness in his voice. "I've been butting heads with the mine and saloon owners since the day that I arrived. They rule the politics, or at least they did until I finally managed to shift things around a little."

Longarm leaned back in his own chair. "Meaning?"

"Meaning that I was fired about fourteen months ago." Kane's lips twisted downward with contempt. "Can you imagine that! They fired me. Said that they no longer had a need for my professional services."

"But you've obviously stayed and even kept a deputy," Longarm said. "How?"

"I went private," Kane said.

Longarm blinked and did not understand. "Meaning?"

"Meaning I provide a service to the people for a fee.

98

A very *modest* fee that pays my salary and that of my deputy.''

Longarm had never heard of such a thing. "And the politicians and businessmen in Bodie went along with this?"

"Hell, no!" Hec declared. "They tried to run us out of town. They even hired a new marshal, but we made sure that he didn't last any longer than the ones before him."

Longarm rubbed his fingers across his eyes. "So you're telling me that neither one of you were elected or even serve at the pleasure of the town council?"

"That's right. Not anymore."

Longarm came to his feet and began to pace back and forth, his mind in no small amount of turmoil. "This is the *town's* jail and office, is it not?"

"Oh, yeah," Kane said. "And I pay them a monthly rent, just like any businessman would."

"But you're *not* a businessman," Longarm said pointedly. "You're the marshal and the man in charge of keeping the peace."

"Don't tell him his damned job," Hec Ward warned. "He knows it better'n you ever will."

"Listen to me, Custis," Kane said, obviously trying to be patient. "I already explained to you how our Boot Hill is filled with men that thought they were smart and tough enough to be Bodie's town marshal."

"Yeah, but—"

"So there came a point where I knew that I had to be tougher and smarter than all the others. I had to do things that . . . well, didn't sit right with folks. I hired Hec to watch my back and to give me a hand. And then when we finally crushed the worst elements in Bodie, the cowardly town council up and decided that we were being a little too hard on folks and that our services were no longer wanted or needed.''

"And that's when you went into business for yourselves.''

"That's right,'' Kane said. "You see, if Hec and I would have handed over our badges and just ridden away, Bodie would have returned to being as lawless as it was before I arrived. All of my work would have been for nothing. My town would have become . . . simply a jungle. A place where only the fittest would be able to survive.''

"He had no choice,'' Hec Ward growled. "Anyone could see that.''

"So,'' Longarm asked, "where does Henry Olliver tie into this story?''

"Olliver was a misfit,'' Kane said with a tolerant smile. "His father owned a blacksmith shop, but then the old man got drunk and got shot. Olliver sold the blacksmith shop and decided to become a preacher.''

Kane laughed with contempt. "Custis, can you even imagine that? In *this* town, a preacher?''

"I've seen some very bad towns that had two or three churches,'' Longarm grimly replied.

Kane's smile died. "Well, maybe you have, but we don't have them in Bodie. And anyway, we're all that is keeping the peace here. This town is like a bucket of poison ready to boil over. We keep a lid on things.''

"You didn't finish the story about Olliver.''

"Oh, yeah,'' Kane said. "Well, when some of the rougher elements in town got drunk and decided that they didn't want a church and a preacher in Bodie, they beat Henry Olliver half to death. Broke his jaw and his nose and a couple of ribs.''

"Three ribs,'' Hec said. "Broke the jaw in two places.

Olliver lost a lot of weight last year.''

''That's right,'' Kane said, ''he did. Anyway, he wanted me to arrest his attackers. Trouble was, they jumped him from behind and he never saw their faces. He thought he could identify them but he had no proof. You've heard all this before, Custis. Probable suspects can't be tried in court without hard evidence.''

Longarm nodded.

''Olliver must have sustained some brain damage during the beating because he started accusing everyone of trying to kill him. Even me!''

''Me too,'' Hec grunted.

''And so he became sort of the town lunatic,'' Kane said. ''He'd preach hellfire and brimstone on the street corners. He'd go into the whorehouses over on Bonanza Street and preach to them ladies of the night too. He became a big nuisance, and I'd have to lock him up for his own protection sometimes.''

''Seems to me,'' Longarm said, ''that a nuisance is just that—a nuisance. Not someone that you expect to see gunned down.''

''Olliver was starting to rouse the town against the saloons and the whorehouses,'' Kane said. ''He'd found some crazy followers and they were becoming pretty vocal. He was causing things to start festering. I tried to protect him, but it was impossible.''

''So that's who you think shot him down last night? A saloon owner or madam?''

''Not a madam, but one of the toughs they hire to police their whorehouses. Hec and I make daily visits to those places and try to keep the peace, but there's always trouble.''

''And you do this for a fee? These visits, I mean,'' Longarm said quietly.

"Well," Kane said, winking. "We sometimes take our fees out in trade. Don't we, Hec?"

The big, brutish deputy guffawed, and Longarm walked over to the window and stared out at the street, trying to put his feelings into words. It wasn't easy.

"What's the matter, Custis? You seem upset about something?"

"I am," he said, turning around to face the two lawmen. "What seems to be wrong here is that you've both forgotten that the law is a *public* issue and concern. It shouldn't just be for those that can afford your fees! Everyone should be protected. Rich and poor. Ivan, this town needs a public lawman. Not a fee collector."

Kane's face drained of color, and Hec Ward's big shoulders humped and black eyes flashed with disgust as he said, "I guess you didn't hear Marshal Kane. Either that, or you weren't listening. We *are* the law in Bodie because no one else can stay alive doing it."

"You're wrong," Longarm said. "There are men who can and will do it. This town had one once."

Longarm looked right at Kane, and the older man's lips pulled back from his teeth when he spat, "You've had your say and we've had our say. I guess this meeting is over."

"I guess it is," Longarm said.

"And you'll be leaving Bodie today," Kane said.

"No, I will not."

Both Kane and Ward came to their feet, and it was the deputy who said, "You look smarter than that. I'd be leaving town, Long."

Longarm looked at one and then the other before he said, "I'm sorry that it's going to have to be this way. I will, of course, have to let Billy Vail know exactly what is going on here in Bodie."

"You let him know anything that you want," Kane said, "but you just let him know from somewhere else. Is that perfectly clear?"

"Yeah," Longarm said, heading for the door and adding on his way out, "I just don't see how it could have been made much clearer."

Chapter 10

When Megan returned to the Kirkwood Livery Stable, she was pleased to see that Mr. Kirkwood had made good on his promise to take excellent care of her two sorrel horses.

"Good morning, Mr. Kirkwood!"

He was cleaning a stall and when he heard Megan's voice, he looked up and a smile creased his face. "Mornin', miss. You have a good night's sleep?"

Megan had a wicked impulse to be honest and tell the man that she had hardly slept at all because she and Custis Long had made love off and on through the entire night.

"Just fine. How are my horses?"

"Just fine too," the man said. "I grained and brushed 'em this morning when my stable boy didn't show up again. Lazy little fart. It's hard to get good help. Hell, I pay the kid a nickel a morning!"

"Hmm," Megan mused aloud while going over to scratch her mare's forehead and then slipping her a cube of sugar that she had gotten at the cafe. Then she did the same for the gelding that Longarm had ridden into Bodie. "Maybe you ought to fire the kid and find another."

"Ain't a lot of kids in Bodie," the man explained.

"There aren't more than a few dozen families and their kids are all spoiled, generally the sons and daughters of mine owners or superintendents. Everything costs too much here for a workingman to bring his family."

"I suppose that's true."

"Lots on Main Street go for about a thousand dollars. I paid only three hundred for the land that this stable sits on, but I could sell it for about two thousand easy."

"And retire in comfort," Megan said, thinking that Kirkwood looked awfully weary and stooped for his age. "Maybe it's something that you ought to consider. You know, these mining towns come and go pretty fast. Could be, if the ore ever gives out here, your land and even this nice stable won't be worth much more than the price of kindling wood."

"You got a good point there," Kirkwood admitted, putting down his pitchfork and mopping his brow because the morning was already warm and the air inside the barn was still. "But the thing of it is that real estate in this town has been rising for the past six years and the mines seem strong. Besides, I don't know where else I'd go that I'd like any better."

"Then stay and enjoy it," Megan said, strolling about in the stable and taking a good look at the horses being boarded.

There were about fifty in corrals outside, but they would be the rough stock, the lesser-quality animals whose owners didn't care if they fought and were kicked in the legs causing shin splints and awful bone problems. The horses with some breeding and quality would always be found in separate stalls, and that's where Megan was looking now.

"What are you looking at?" Kirkwood asked.

"Just seeing what kinds of horses people keep in Bodie."

"There some damned good ones," Kirkwood assured her. "And I own a few of 'em."

"Really?"

"That's right." Kirkwood forgot about finishing cleaning the stall. "Come over here and look at this palomino."

Megan followed the man, and watched as he opened the stall and stepped inside. A moment later, he was leading a very handsome horse out for her inspection.

"Ain't he something, though?"

"He's a dandy, all right," Megan agreed. "Where'd you get him?"

"He belonged to a gambler who was shot and killed after he got caught dealing from the bottom of the deck. The man owed everyone in town, but he owed me the most. So I paid off the others and took the horse."

"I'm sure that you got a wonderful deal," Megan said. "You probably got him cheap."

"Not so cheap as you might think," Kirkwood said. "I guess I'm out about two hundred dollars for him."

"My, my! He isn't *that* nice."

Kirkwood's eyes dilated. "What do you mean! He can run like the wind and never get tired. He's intelligent— if you knew much about horses you could see that in his eyes."

Megan smiled sweetly. "Why, I can see that is a fine animal, but a horse like that would only bring about a hundred dollars in Reno. And that, Mr. Kirkwood, would be the absolute tops."

Kirkwood visibly deflated. "Really?"

"I'm afraid so."

"Well," the man blustered, "he's worth at least twice

that in Bodie. I mean to enter him in a race one of these days and win a bundle of money.''

Megan nodded as if she believed this, but then said, ''I just hope that the race you enter him in is short.''

''Why?'' Kirkwood asked suspiciously.

''Why? Because it's obvious that he's been wind-broke. I doubt he'd be able to run more than a few hundred yards before he'd be gasping and wheezing.''

''That's crazy! Why, this horse is as sound as a dollar.''

''A *Confederate* dollar, maybe,'' Megan said, going to look at the other horses. ''You own any of these?''

Kirkwood put the palomino back into its stall. He looked upset and distracted.

''This mare looks to be . . . what, about twenty years old?''

Kirkwood glanced up suddenly. ''Ten!'' he snapped. ''I've owned her two years and she wasn't even eight then.''

''Oh, no,'' Megan said, shaking her head and smiling sadly. ''This mare is *ancient* and I do mean that. I'd say she was on the sundown side of twenty, at least.''

''What makes you think so?''

''The way her teeth are parroting out. Not only do their teeth get worn down flat so that there are no cups, but they begin to point or 'parrot' outward. And look at the depth of those sockets over her eyes. And see how her—''

''All right, dammit! Maybe she is older than ten. But she's not twenty, dammit!''

''I'm quite certain that she's real old,'' Megan said, stroking the mare's muzzle.

''Look at this one,'' Kirkwood thundered, marching over to throw open a stall door and yank a fine-looking bay mare out by her halter. He grinned triumphantly. ''I dare you to fault this handsome mare.''

Megan put her hands on her hips and then walked around the mare twice. She was about fifteen hands and just under a thousand pounds. Straight-legged with an excellent conformation. Her hooves were black and looked hard as diamonds, and when Megan studied her legs, they were straight and long.

"Well?" Kirkwood demanded.

"Not bad," Megan said. "I'm sure that she'll make a fine ladies' horse."

"Ladies' horse!" the stableman thundered. "Why, she's horse enough for any *man*."

"A little light-boned for the average-sized man," Megan argued. "But she looks like she could run."

"The man I bought her from said she'd outrun everything in Aurora last fall and made him a lot of money. I ain't raced her in Bodie, but I will some day."

"I'd race her before I'd race that wind-broke palomino you paid way too much for," Megan said.

Kirkwood reached for his chewing tobacco and crammed a big wad into his mouth. He chewed hard and fast. "So you like this mare, huh?"

"I do."

"How much is she worth to you?"

Megan took her time and acted as if she had to struggle to come up with her best figure. "Maybe forty dollars."

Kirkwood scoffed. "Why, you're worse than a bank thief! I paid sixty and I stole her."

"If you find a woman that can handle that much horse, you might get your money out of her," Megan said, starting to turn away.

"Wait a minute! Could *you* handle her?"

"Yes." Megan eyed the mare. "She's strong-willed, though, isn't she."

"Yeah," the man said. "I got the boy to saddle and try to ride her, but she pitched the kid off and he hurt his shoulder. He won't ride her anymore, and I'm too busted up from other horses to risk getting pitched. I've been looking for someone to ride her out. I don't suppose that you . . ."

"I'll buy her from you for forty dollars cash," Megan said.

"No, miss, I won't do that."

"Then you'll be feeding the mare for a long, long time, Mr. Kirkwood."

Megan went over to the mare, and the horse rolled her eyes and snorted, a clear indication that she had been mistreated by someone and was afraid of humans.

It was all that Kirkwood could do to hold her down, and when she lashed out at him with a forefoot, he shouted and released the halter crying, "Whoa, damn you!"

Megan dashed to the barn door and shut it before the mare could escape. Then, she took some more sugar cubes out of her pockets and began to talk to the bay mare while slowly moving in her direction.

The mare bolted and ran around inside the barn a couple of times, but Megan just kept talking and walking. Pretty soon, she was able to get a hold of the mare's halter.

"See," she crooned as the mare's jaws pulverized sugar cubes, "that wasn't so bad, was it?"

"You got a way with 'er," Kirkwood said, folding his arms across his narrow chest. "I'll have to admit that much. I'd like to see you ride the mare out, though."

"Forty dollars cash and I'll give you another twenty dollars for the palomino."

110

"Twenty!" Kirkwood screamed. "I told you that I paid two hundred."

"Sometimes," Megan said, "a person just has to swallow their losses and move on to bigger and better deals. Unless you know Paiute horse medicine like I do, Mr. Kirkwood, you're just going to be throwing more good money after bad with that wind-broke palomino."

"I think you're trying to cheat me! That's what I think you are trying to do, young woman!"

"Then let's saddle and run him around a little," Megan said. "Where's a saddle?"

"Whoa! If what you say is true, then everyone in Bodie would see what a fool I was to spend so much money on that gambler's horse. Why, I'd be the laughingstock of the town. I can't afford that, being as I'm supposed to be the horse man around here."

"Well," Megan said, "you need to know that I'm telling you the truth about this horse. That it *is* wind-broke and it's going to take some work and Indian medicine to restore the animal to its natural healthy state."

Kirkwood removed his hat and ran his fingers through his rapidly thinning hair. "So," he said at last, "you're offering me just sixty dollars for the two finest-looking animals in Bodie."

"One being wind-broke and the other half wild and slightly undersized."

"Damn!" Kirkwood swore. "There's just no doubt that you're trying to skin me."

"Then don't take my money," Megan said, pulling it out of her pocket and counting out sixty dollars. "I'm sure that there are plenty of other horses to buy in Bodie."

"None as pretty as that pair."

"Sixty-five and that's my limit," Megan said. "Take it or leave it."

"I'll take it."

"And throw in the board bills for my sorrels plus these two for one full week."

"No!"

"The board bill for five days and I do a day's saddle repair work for you free."

"You're a saddle maker too?"

"I am."

"Man, oh, man," Kirkwood said, "you are one of a kind, young lady."

"Do we have a deal?"

Kirkwood muttered something under his breath, but he took her money and then said, "I'll write you out a couple of bills of sale and show you the saddle work that needs doing."

Megan was pleased with herself. She'd not lied to Kirkwood. The mare *was* spooked, but mostly when it came to men. With plenty of attention and kindness, the mare would be a peach of a horse for someone, and Megan even had a few possibilities in mind. She thought that she might be able to double her money on the bay mare, especially if she looked to be the short-track sprinter that she appeared to be.

The palomino was another matter entirely. He was wind-broken, but horses like that could be cured by the Paiutes, who claimed that they did so by burning a medicinal mix of sagebrush, pine nuts, and several other secret ingredients and then forcing the horse to inhale this healing smoke. Megan had seen them cure horses like this one before, and she knew that there was a very good chance that the Paiute medicine men could cure this handsome palomino, whose breathing was slightly labored even as he stood at rest.

The two saddles that Kirkwood wanted repaired would take no more than a couple of hours.

"So tell me about Marshal Kane," she said, giving the stable man a disarming smile. "Is he honest, or is he extorting the good businessmen of this town like yourself out of a lot of protection money?"

"I'd rather not talk about the sonofabitch," Kirkwood snapped. "Talking about Marshal Kane just isn't the healthy thing to do in Bodie."

"I see." Megan studied the badly abused saddle and acted like she did not even hear Kirkwood's response. "So what about all the rumors that he is bleeding this town and shooting down people rather than arresting them and seeing them brought to trial."

"His deputy is as bad as Marshal Kane. Worse, in fact."

"I haven't yet met the man."

"Name is Hec Ward, and he's a bloodthirsty bastard that would as soon shoot a man as give him a hello."

"I see."

"No," Kirkwood said, "you *don't* see until you've watched that pair in action when they collect their fees."

"Do you pay him?"

Kirkwood lowered his chin to his chest. "I didn't want to," he whispered. "At first I held out like some of the others. Then things started happening to my horses and stuff. Next thing I knew, there was a note on my barn door saying that, if I didn't cooperate, my barn and hay-stack would be burned to the ground. That would wipe me out, Miss Riley."

"And this note came from Marshal Kane?"

"I don't know. He and his deputy would never be stupid enough to show their hand that way. Oh, they'll collect their protection money, but they wouldn't let anyone know it was done under a threat.''

"But you're pretty sure that it was them?''

"Who else stands to gain?''

"No one that I know about," Megan said.

"They're a cancer on this town. It was bad before they came. It's even worse now. But Marshal Kane and his deputy with the hook hand aren't the real powers in this town.''

"They're not?''

"No," Kirkwood said, with a look of satisfaction. "Even *they* have to take their orders.''

"From?''

"I don't know. Maybe some of the mine owners. They're the ones with the most money and power in Bodie.''

"But why would they—''

"To get even more money," Kirkwood said. "Have you ever seen anyone claimed they had enough money?''

"Not outside the clergy.''

"Then I rest my case," Kirkwood said.

Megan went to work repairing the saddles, but her mind was really on Custis and the disturbing news that she had just learned with all of its evil ramifications.

Chapter 11

When Megan finally showed up at their hotel room, Longarm let her in and then locked the door. "Where have you been so long?" he asked.

"At Kirkwood's livery repairing a saddle and buying a couple of horses. Why?"

"I want you to leave town now," Longarm said, sitting her down on the bed. "I want you to ride to Carson City."

"Why!"

"Because it's the nearest telegraph office."

"Who—"

"I want you to send a telegraph to my office in Denver, Megan. It needs to go off as fast as possible."

"I can't leave you here alone!"

"Of course you can," he said firmly. "There's going to be trouble and I may need some help."

"Then that's all the more reason for me to stay!"

"No, it isn't," Longarm argued. "What I really need you to do is to get to Carson City and send off that telegram."

Longarm rustled through his pockets until he found a paper and pencil. "I'll write out exactly what I want you to send."

Megan bounced off the bed. "I can't do this," she said. "I can't run out on you. Mr. Kirkwood told me that this town is ready to explode. That Marshal Kane and his deputy, while they may *think* they're the ones in power, are only fooling themselves. Kirkwood says it's the mine owners that control things here in Bodie."

"I know," Longarm said. "Kane admitted as much. But he said that the miners' union and saloon owners also have a lot of power."

"So who," Megan asked with exasperation, "really does run things in this town?"

"That's the problem," Longarm said. "No one does. There's this big power struggle going on and it's bound to erupt in gunfire and bloodshed. Kane and his deputy, a man named Hec Ward, are trying to act tough, but I think they're really worried."

"They've got every reason to be."

"Megan," Longarm said. "Marshal Kane and Deputy Ward as much as told me that I'd be shot on sight if I didn't take his warning and leave Bodie today."

"Then why don't you! We can ride to Carson City and wait for help."

"That isn't going to help me get to the bottom of all this trouble," Longarm argued. "I've never been scared off before, and I'm not about to be scared off now."

"Use your head, Custis!" Megan cried, throwing her arms around his neck and hugging him tightly. "You *need* help!"

Longarm began to pace back and forth. He knew that Megan was making a lot of sense, and yet . . . and yet it galled him no end to think about retreating from Bodie to seek reinforcements. He had always been proud of being able to handle any situation on his own, and he did not want to see that changed.

116

"We'll leave now," Megan said. "We'll ride to Carson City and send that telegram. How long would it be before you could expect some federal officers?"

"Four or five days."

"Well what difference would that small amount of time make!" Megan exclaimed. "They've been spilling blood in Bodie for years."

Longarm wavered. There was a case to be made for backing off here and returning with help. Even great Civil War generals like Sherman and Grant had often retreated, only to regroup and strike again when the odds were more in their favor.

"You have nothing to prove," Megan was saying as she walked over to the window and then turned to face him. "Getting caught in the middle of some power struggle between the miners' union, the mine operators, the saloon owners, and Marshal Kane simply doesn't make any sense."

"Maybe you're right," Longarm finally conceded. "If they see me leaving town, that might just lull everyone into thinking that I've gotten cold feet. They might get careless and—"

Longarm's words were cut short by the boom of a high-powered rifle and the shattering of their glass hotel window. A shout of warning filled his throat, but even as he jumped toward Megan, he knew that he was too late to protect her.

The impact of the heavy-caliber slug spun her completely around and threw Megan to the floor.

"No!" Longarm shouted, diving to Megan's side.

The wound was ugly and bleeding heavily, but it was not going to be fatal. Longarm saw at once that Megan had been extremely fortunate, that the ambusher had not had a clear view but had fired only at a shadow on their curtain. Megan would live if he could stop the hemorrhaging.

"Oh, dammit!" he shouted, jumping over to the bed and tearing up a sheet. "Megan!"

She was conscious, but already pale. She tried to push herself erect, but he held her to the floor saying, "Just relax and lie still. I'm going to get this bleeding under control and then we'll get you a doctor."

"What . . . what happened?" she whispered as he pressed the bandaging to her shoulder. "Custis, tell me the truth, am I going to *die*?"

"No," he promised. "I swear that you're going to be fine. You were lucky, Megan. It's just a flesh wound. I can't tell yet, but I think the slug passed right on through the muscle and tissue without hitting any bone."

"It's numb," she breathed. "It doesn't even hurt. But I feel cold!"

Longarm pressed the bedding even tighter to the wound. He'd been shot a number of times himself, and he knew the feeling that Megan was experiencing and that the pain would come later.

"Just hold still."

"Who was it?" she whispered. "Who shot me?"

"I don't know," he replied, "but I swear to God that I'll find out."

"Probably the marshal or his deputy."

"Probably."

Longarm checked Megan's pulse, and was not surprised to discover that it was racing. "Megan," he said, "we need to get a doctor up here."

"Do think there is one in Bodie?"

"Yes," he said, "and next to the undertakers, they're likely to be the most prosperous men in town."

Longarm slipped his hand under Megan and said, "I'm

118

going to roll you over easy so that your weight is on this bandage, and then I'm going downstairs to get us some help.''

Megan's eyes dilated and her fingernails bit into his forearm. ''Please,'' she whispered, ''don't leave me. I could bleed to death all alone.''

''All right,'' he said, deciding to carry her downstairs. ''Just loop your arm around my neck and we'll go find a doctor right now.''

Megan nodded. She was extremely pale, and Longarm was scared that she might actually bleed to death before he could get her real medical help. And what if there actually was no legitimate doctor in Bodie? Well, then, Longarm thought, I'll find a needle and thread and sew her up myself.

She grunted with pain when he lifted and carried her out of their hotel room. Longarm descended the stairs carefully, and when he reached the lobby, he shouted at the desk clerk and everyone else in the place.

''This woman has been shot! We need a doctor!''

The desk clerk stared at Megan. ''Oh, dear heavens! Was she shot in your room?''

''Yes, dammit! Someone tried to ambush me through the window and got my wife instead. Now, get a damn doctor over here!''

The clerk bolted out from behind his desk yelling, ''Yes, sir, Mr. Jefferson! Yes, sir!''

Longarm looked down at Megan. Her skin was bathed in a cold sweat and her breathing was shallow and rapid.

''You can lay her over here on this sofa,'' a hotel guest said. ''We got two doctors and neither one of them is worth spit, but I'll go help find 'em.''

''Much obliged,'' Longarm said, laying Megan down

119

on the sofa. He looked up and shouted, "Someone find us blankets!"

There were three other men in the lobby, and they all dashed upstairs to get their own blankets.

"Just hang on," Longarm told Megan, slipping his hand under her shoulder to discover that the bandaging he'd used was saturated with her blood. "Just hang on."

The hotel clerk was the first one back with a doctor in tow. He was a short, heavyset man in his sixties, round and out of breath.

"Goddammit," he stammered, "who the hell is so important that you interrupt . . ."

But when he saw Megan and then felt Longarm's icy gaze, his words died in his throat. "What happened to her?"

"Shot through a window by a high-powered rifle. A Hawken or Sharps, from the sound of the retort," Longarm said tightly. "The slug tore away a big hunk of flesh and might even have scored a rib."

"Has she lost much blood?"

"Of course she has!" Longarm shouted. "Can't you tell just by looking at her?"

The doctor rocked back, face turning crimson. "Don't you dare shout at me! I only had a year of *dentistry* training in Boston! I'm—"

"Get out of here!" Longarm grated. "Anyone who would ask as stupid a question as that after seeing this girl has no right to practice medicine."

The man jumped back. "She'll bleed to death if I don't help her! Twenty dollars, cash up front."

Longarm was so outraged and infuriated that, had it not been for Megan needing him at her side, he would have jumped up and throttled the little sonofabitch with his bare hands. "Get out of here!"

The man spun on his heels and headed for the door, almost colliding with Bodie's other doctor. This man was older and far more dignified-looking. However, he had the red, heavily veined nose of a bad drinker and when he drew closer, Longarm could see that his eyes were bloodshot and unclear.

"Are you drunk!" Longarm demanded.

"Not yet." The man straightened and lifted his chin. He was thin and his clothes were threadbare, his cuffs frayed and soiled. He held a medical bag in his bony hand, and was gripping it so tightly that his knuckles were white.

"This girl's shoulder was laid open by a big-caliber hunting rifle," Longarm said. "She's still hemorrhaging although I've done everything I can to stanch the flow. Can you help her?"

"Sir?"

"You had better be sober and good enough to help her," Longarm warned. "Because if you're not and you touch her, I'll make sure that you never touch another patient."

The tall man gulped. "Is that a . . . a threat?" he whispered.

"No, a promise."

For a moment, Longarm was sure that the man was going to turn and run to his next drink. But then, he seemed to gather himself and stand even taller to pronounce, "I was, sir, a captain in the Union army, and I've treated hundreds . . . no, thousands of gunshot and saber wounds. So stand aside!"

Longarm had never been happier to stand aside. He could smell whiskey on the doctor's breath and the man's hands were shaking slightly, but otherwise, he seemed in full control of his faculties.

"How much blood has this young lady lost?"

"Too much," Longarm said, watching as the doctor lifted one of Megan's eyelids, then the other to measure the size of her pupils. He then took her pulse.

"Shallow and racing," he pronounced. "We've got to get the hemorrhaging under control very quickly."

"I know that."

The doctor ordered Longarm to roll Megan over so that he could examine her injury. When Longarm did, he saw the doctor's eyes widen with obvious alarm.

"This is a nasty wound," the doctor said, tearing open his medical bag and pulling out a kit of suturing needles, thread, and bandages. "She's already in shock and I may not be able to save her, but I'll try."

"That's all that I expect."

The doctor tried to thread his needle, but his hands were shaking too badly, so Longarm did it for him while the man fumbled into his pocket and extracted a pint of whiskey.

"To steady the nerves," he said when Longarm started to grab the bottle away from him.

"All right, but just for the nerves," Longarm warned.

"Of course." The man took a long pull on the bottle, then corked it and said, "By the way, my name is Thaddeus Blake. Dr. Thaddeus Blake."

"And you've had training?"

"Yes," the man said, slipping the bottle into his pocket and bending over Megan so that he could began his work.

"First," Blake said, dousing his hands with a little of the whiskey and then gently easing his forefinger into the wound. "I must be sure that there are no fragments of lead in her body."

"Shouldn't you use forceps?"

122

"Probably," Blake said, "but I prefer my own methods."

Longarm held his breath, and Thaddeus Blake actually closed his suffering eyes so that he could concentrate better on his fingertip.

"Ah," he grunted softly, "the slug is still inside of her."

"Can you . . ."

"There," Thaddeus whispered, "I've got it!"

And sure enough, the doctor did extract the misshapen hunk of lead, saying, "It's obscene, isn't it, what a small piece of lead can do the human tissue."

"It's not that small," Longarm told him.

"Give me the needle and suture," Blade ordered, his face now bathed in the sweat of his own fevered anxiety. "I am quite sure that this lovely young girl cannot stand this blood loss for more than a few more minutes."

Megan flinched the first time the curved needle entered her torn flesh, but then she mercifully fainted. Longarm kept sponging away blood so that the doctor could see where he was stitching.

"You've also done this a time or two before, haven't you," Blake muttered as his brow was creased with intense concentration.

"That's right." Longarm studied the man. Thaddeus Blake might have been sixty, but Longarm was willing to bet that he was, in actuality, at least ten years younger. Sweat was beading on his forehead and he looked very unwell.

"Do you need more whiskey to steady yourself, Doctor?"

"Yes!" Blake almost cried.

Because the doctor's hands were all bloody and filled with needle and suture, Longarm had to reach into the man's pocket and extract the bottle again, then uncork it and put it to Blake's lips. The surgeon threw back his head and gulped four times.

"Ahh! Thank you!"

"Mind if I finish the bottle?" Longarm asked. "There isn't much left and I could use some for my own nerves."

"By all means, help yourself!"

Longarm emptied the bottle, but was immediately sorry. The whiskey was raw and burned a river of fire right down to his belly. It was about as bad as horse piss.

"Jezus!" Longarm choked. "Doc, you gotta start drinking something else. That stuff will kill you!"

"No one lives forever," Thaddeus Blake replied.

"Hell of an attitude for a doctor to take," Longarm growled.

Blake mopped his brow with the back of his sleeve and kept suturing. His work wasn't the prettiest that Longarm had ever seen, but it was effective and the bleeding was already greatly diminished.

"How come you want to kill yourself, Doc?"

"Long, boring story that you don't want to hear," the man replied. "Who is this girl?"

"My friend."

"Your lady friend shouldn't have come to Bodie."

"I know."

"She's going to live," the doctor said, "but she won't be able to travel for at least two weeks. Move her even by stage or private buggy and you would run the risk of these sutures breaking loose. It's going to take her months to fully regain her strength."

"She lives in Reno."

"She should have stayed in Reno instead of coming to this hellish place," Dr. Blake flatly stated.

Longarm felt terrible. Here he was being crowded on

all sides by enemies, and now he had Megan to worry about. And if he were gunned down in ambush, what would become of her until such time as she was able to leave Bodie? Just the thought of Megan Riley being bedridden and at the mercy of this town was enough to make Longarm curse the decision he'd made to allow her to accompany him. What in heaven's name had he been thinking of at the time?

"We're done," the doctor said. "I suggest we get her up to your room."

Longarm glanced over his shoulder and yelled at the desk clerk, "We're going to need a new room!"

"Yes, sir, Mr. Jefferson!" A minute passed and then the clerk hurried over with a key in his fist. "Room 206, but I'll have to charge you for the damages, cleaning, and . . ."

Something in Longarm's eyes killed the man's wheedling voice. He dropped the new room key on the carpet and hurried away.

"I guess," the doctor said, "that after we get this girl to bed you owe me some money."

"I guess that I do," Longarm said, "and I'm more than happy to pay your fee."

Thaddeus Blake smiled and wiped his hands on a blanket. "I will stay with her for a short while," he announced. "But I'll need some more . . . medicine."

"And you shall have it," Longarm promised as he lifted the unconscious Megan up again and carried her back toward the stairs.

Chapter 12

"All right, goddammit!" Longarm swore as he barged into Marshal Kane's office and caught the two lawmen off guard with their feet up on their desks. "Who tried to kill me and shot Miss Riley instead!"

Kane's jaw dropped, and then the heels of his boots hit the floor as he bounced up to his feet. "Did someone shoot Miss Riley?"

"That's right." Longarm whirled to face Deputy Hec Ward. "You warned me to get out of town. Maybe you didn't want to take a chance I'd call your play."

Ward jumped to his feet, eyes blazing. "I don't ambush women! I don't have to ambush anyone, damn you!"

The outraged Hec Ward stabbed for his gun, but Longarm had anticipated the move and the butt of his Colt was already planted solidly in his fist. Longarm's Colt was a blur as its muzzle locked on the one-armed deputy's chest.

Ward froze, eyes bugging. For a moment, no one in the office moved, and then Longarm said, "I don't like you, Deputy Ward, but I'm not convinced that you're a backshooter."

Longarm's eyes snapped over to Marshal Kane, who

had not moved a muscle. "Why don't you and your trigger-happy deputy both raise your hands over your heads," Longarm growled.

"Why should we?" Kane demanded.

"Because," Longarm said, "I'm placing you both under arrest until I get to the bottom of things around here and restore some order."

Kane's face mottled with rage. "You're putting *me* under arrest!"

"That's right. As a federal officer—"

"As a federal officer, you have *no authority* in my town!" the lawman shouted.

"And as someone who admits he has been fired by the Bodie town council, you have even less authority here than I do," Longarm said, gun slowly shifting from one to the other. "Now, I don't know what is going to happen next, Marshal Kane. It's entirely up to you. But I'm telling you to get your hands in the air and turn around slow."

"I'll kill you for this," Kane vowed between clenched teeth. "You've no right to arrest us!"

"I'll worry about that later," Longarm said. "Now turn around, put your hands over your heads, and if you reach for your guns or a hideout, I'll not hesitate to split your skulls wide open with the barrel of my gun."

"You sonofabitch!" Ward screamed as he turned around and obeyed the order.

Longarm had a few tense moments as he searched and then disarmed the dangerous pair.

"All right," he said, "it's time to get a dose of your own medicine."

"You're making a hell of a bad mistake," Kane said. "A *fatal* mistake."

"This may come as a shock to you, Ivan," Longarm said as he herded them both into the jail cell and locked the door, "but people have told me that before."

"This time it'll happen," Kane said, turning around and studying him. "I liked you, Marshal Long. I thought you had some common sense."

"Meaning?"

"Meaning that someone else was trying to kill you. It wasn't us. And that being the case, you haven't got a clue as to who is trying to put a hole in your hide."

"At least I know who *won't* be," Longarm said, looking right at Hec Ward.

"There's something else you should know," Kane said. "When word gets out that we are disarmed and in this cell, we're both dead men. They'll shoot us in here like we were fish in a barrel."

"They might try," Longarm said, "but I'll be close."

"What about Miss Riley?"

"What about her?"

"You going to be close to her as well," Kane asked, "just in case it *wasn't* an accident that she got ambushed?"

Longarm frowned. "Why would anyone deliberately try to kill Megan?"

Kane shrugged. He seemed surprisingly calm, given the circumstances. "I don't know," he finally admitted. "But her father is a well-known lawman. A lot of people in this part of the country hate his guts and would like to do anything they could to bring him pain. Even shooting his daughter."

"If they wanted to do that, they could have done it far easier in Reno," Longarm countered. "That doesn't make any sense at all to me."

"Listen to me well," Kane said. "You're in way over your head. Hec and me were barely treading water, trying to figure out who is out to put us down under and is

129

shaking down some of the merchants.''

Longarm laughed coldly. "I *know* who that is and it's you," he said.

When Kane looked away suddenly, Longarm turned his back on the pair and went to the front door. Before opening it, he said, "I'm taking the jail cell keys with me, and if you don't make a big fuss, no one will find out what happened in here."

"You can't keep this a secret!" Ward swore. "Goddamn you, Long, the word will be out in ten minutes and we'll be dead in fifteen."

Longarm noted the panic in Ward's voice right alongside the anger and outrage. And as he closed the door behind him, he made sure that it was locked and he had the key. Satisfied that no one could get into the marshal's office, Longarm hurried back to the U.S. Hotel to check on Megan, hoping that he hadn't made a big, big mistake.

Megan opened her eyes after listening to Longarm describe how he had jailed Kane and Ward. She took a deep breath and said, "You've *got* to get some help."

"I know that."

Longarm reached into his vest pocket and produced a piece of paper. "I'm going to give this to one of the passengers who are boarding the stage this afternoon and ask him to take it to the telegraph office in Carson City. They'll send the message to Denver and I'll get help."

"Yes, but how long will that take?" Megan reached out and took Longarm's hand. She looked extremely worried. "Custis, it might take a week before your boss can get some help over here. You could be *dead* by then."

"I'm not easy to kill."

Megan sighed. Her color was so much better and she looked as if she might be able to get up and start walking around in a day or two. The doctor had said that the wound in her shoulder would leave an unsightly scar, but that she should again have full use of her arm and shoulder.

"Why don't you load me up in a buggy or even a buckboard and take me back home to Reno. My father . . ."

"Is half blind and he'd be half crazy when he saw what I'd let happen to you. Megan, I got enough troubles right now without also worrying about your father trying to carry out his threat to shoot my balls off. Do you remember that pleasant little warning?"

"I remember. All right, so what are you going to do?"

"I don't know," Longarm confessed. "I'm concerned about you, but also about Marshal Kane. He says that someone will surely try and kill him and his deputy if I leave them unprotected in their jail cell."

"He's just trying to get you to let him go so he can shoot you, Custis. I'm sure of it."

"I dunno anymore," Longarm said. "Over the years, I've become a pretty good judge of when someone is lying to me and when they're being honest. And I can tell you right now that Kane is genuinely scared that someone is going to poke a gun through that jail cell window and gun him and the deputy down."

"Maybe you'd better go to the stage station and send that telegram," Megan suggested. "It sounds to me like we've got a wildcat by the tail."

"We do," Longarm said. "Megan, I'm really sorry about you getting shot on my account. The surgeon who took a slug out of you said that you were extremely lucky that no major artery was severed. Even so, you almost bled to death. And you're going to have a scar."

"That's not so important, is it?" she asked softly, her

eyes misting a little. "I mean, you'll still think I'm . . . well, nice to make love to. Won't you?"

Longarm nodded. "Any man would."

"It's not any man that I care about," she said. "It's just you and my father."

"We'll be all right," Longarm said, stretching out on the bed beside her. "I need to think things out a few minutes, and then I'll go on over to the stage line and find someone to carry that telegraph message to the operator in Carson City."

"Sure," Megan said.

Longarm stretched out beside the young woman. "Does it hurt pretty bad?"

"I've been kicked and stepped on, and once I had a stallion take a big bite out of my butt," Megan told him. "*That* hurt a lot worse than this."

"You almost bled to death."

"Shhh!"

Longarm closed his eyes. Things had been moving so fast that he really did need to think his next move out. He needed to turn everything over a couple of times in his head to make sure that sending a telegraph off was the right thing to do. At the moment it seemed the only thing to do, but Longarm had learned from hard experience that a man had to hold something up and examine it from all angles just to make sure that he wasn't making some major mistake.

He must have fallen asleep.

"Custis!"

His eyes popped open. Megan was staring at him, wide-eyed. "Custis," she repeated. "There's a terrible commotion going on downstairs."

She was right. Longarm heard shouts and then the sound of boots pounding on the staircase. He heard them thunder up the hallway and stop at his door.

"Open up, Jefferson!"

Longarm rolled off the bed. "How long was I asleep?"

"No more than thirty minutes. I was going to wake you in—"

"Jefferson, open the damn door!"

"Oh, my God," Longarm breathed as, gun clenched in his fist, he rushed toward their locked door. "I think they've shot Kane and his deputy."

Longarm's guess was right. When he opened the door, he had only to take one quick look at the crowd of faces to see that a shocking thing had taken place in Bodie.

"You put them in that jail cell, didn't you!" a heavyset man demanded. "I saw you leave and lock the office door. And then some murderin' bastard sneaked up to the alley window, stuck his gun through the bars, and riddled 'em both."

"We heard 'em screaming," another man said, accusation thick in his voice.

"Listen," Longarm said, "I put them there, but—"

"Goddammit, let's hang him!" a man shouted.

Longarm knew that the crowd was too shocked and filled with emotion to listen to reason. Ivan Kane and Hec Ward had been feared and even despised by most of the citizens, but they had been gunned down. Shot like fish in a barrel. The people of Bodie were shocked and outraged. Nothing but hanging Longarm would satisfy them in their present state of mind.

The gun was already in Longarm's fist, and he wasn't going to hand it over to this lynch mob without taking a few men with him, if need be. He fired a slug into the carpet between them and the mob fell back, some knocking others down in their panic to retreat.

"Listen to me," he shouted. "I didn't shoot them!

133

Someone else did, and they'll get off scot-free unless I get to the bottom of these shootings.''

"You've done enough already!" a big man with a red mustache shouted as he surged forward.

Longarm slashed him across the bridge of the nose with his Colt. The man cried out in pain and cupped his face in his big hands, blood pouring from his broken nose. Longarm cocked back the hammer of his gun.

"I'm a federal officer of the law," he loudly announced. "My name isn't Thomas Jefferson, it's Custis Long, and I'm a deputy United States marshal."

"If you're a U.S. marshal you got no business here in Bodie!" a man in the back of the crowd yelled.

"I've got all the authority I need," Longarm shouted, using his left hand to dig his badge out of his pocket and hold it up to the crowd. "This town has a federally chartered bank and it's been robbed. It has federal mail that has been stolen as well. That gives me all the authority that I need."

The crowd had lost its zeal and blood lust. They were staring at the big man with all the blood running between his fingers and they did not want the same punishment.

"Now then," Longarm said, closing and locking the door behind him to block the view of Megan. "I want sworn statements from the first people to reach the bodies."

"I don't think Marshal Kane is quite dead yet," one man offered.

Longarm had been about to say something, but now he gaped. "Are you sure!"

"Well, he might be dead by now," the man said, "but he was still alive when Dr. Blake got to him."

Longarm didn't wait to hear any more. He elbowed men aside in his haste to get down the hallway to the stairs. He took the stairs three at a time, and sprinted across the lobby and outside. There was another large crowd blocking the entrance to the marshal's office, and someone had been forced to hack the door open with an ax.

"Step aside!" Longarm shouted. "Everyone step aside!"

When they were slow to move, Longarm drew his gun and fired two shots into the sky. The crowd parted, and he rushed into the office and saw Dr. Blake in the cell kneeling beside Ivan Kane. When Blake saw Longarm, he said, "Good thing I had a key to this cell or he'd have bled to death before anyone could have reached him."

"You mean he's going to live?"

"No," the doctor said. "He's taken a bullet through the gut and another through the lung. But he's still alive. He wants to talk to someone named Marshal Long."

"That's me," Longarm said. He knelt beside the dying lawman and shook his head back and forth, almost overwhelmed with remorse. "I'm sorry, Ivan. I . . . I'm just sorry as hell."

Ivan grabbed his wrist. "It's all right," he whispered, a wheezing, gurgling sound coming from the bullet hole through his lung. "Maybe better this way."

"Who did it?"

Ivan's grip was surprisingly strong and a shout was torn from his blood-frothy lips. "Jack Ramey!"

"I'll find him," Longarm promised. "I'll see him hang for this."

The marshal's breathing was shallow and rapid. He was struggling hard but drowning in his own blood. "Hired by . . . by them."

"By who?"

Kane's eyes grew round, and he stared at the fly-specked ceiling as if he finally glimpsed into eternity.

"Oh, by . . . by God!" he choked.

Kane's body began to shiver as a mighty convulsion shook him. Longarm grabbed the man by the shoulders and tried to hold him still, but it was hopeless. He had seen too many men die before. Then Kane let out a cry, rattled his boot heels across the floor several times, and died.

Longarm expelled a deep breath. Slowly, he climbed to his feet and said, "You heard him, Doc. He said the man that shot him is named Jack Ramey."

"He's a gunman, all right. Shouldn't be hard to find unless he's already cut and run."

"Where does he hang out at?"

"The Champion Saloon."

"I know where it's at," Longarm said.

"If you go in there, you'd better keep that gun in your hand, because there are a lot of rough men in there," the doctor warned. "Jack Ramey is just one of the professionals, but he isn't even the worst of the lot."

"Who do they work for?"

"Whoever is willing to pay 'em the best money," the doctor replied. "Sometimes they just ride out for a month or two and when they come back, they're usually flush. I expect they rob stagecoaches, banks, and anyone that looks like they got a few dollars on their person."

Longarm knew the type well. He moved over to the body of Hec Ward. The man had been shot at least four times, mostly in the back. He was still in a kneeling position, head pressed to the bars, hand and hook circling them. It was a pathetic sight and a miserable way for such a tough and dangerous man to die.

"Almost looks like he'd found the Lord as he was dying, don't it?" someone said.

"No," Longarm answered, "it just looks to me like

Hec Ward was trying to rip the bars out of the floor and run away.''

"He was a hard man hisself.''

"Yeah,'' Longarm said, unclenching Ward's hand and then removing his hook from the bars. When he rolled the deputy over, he could see that Ward had bitten through his own tongue in fear or in pain. The man's mouth was filled with congealing blood, and the sight was so grisly that Longarm suddenly looked away.

"I think,'' Dr. Blake said, "I've seen about all the carnage I can stand for one day.''

Longarm felt the same, but headed for the Champion Saloon anyway.

Chapter 13

Longarm was in a dangerous mood as he marched up the street, eyes riveted straight ahead. He doubted that Ramey or his friends would be expecting trouble because it seemed impossible that anyone could have survived even a few minutes in that jail cell. In all probability, Jack Ramey was convinced that he had assassinated Marshal Kane and his deputy without being seen and that he would never be held accountable for his bloody and murderous deed.

Four doors down from the Champion Saloon, Longarm halted on the boardwalk and turned to look inside a gunsmith's shop. The owner was staring at him, obviously sensing trouble.

"Do you know Jack Ramey?" Longarm asked, stepping just inside the shop.

"Maybe."

The gunsmith was in his forties, a hard-bitten fellow with a deep saber or knife scar etched across his right cheek. He was also missing a couple of fingers. The stub of an unlit nickel cigar protruded from his yellow teeth, and he cradled an old .36-caliber Navy Colt in his hands.

"Maybe you'd better start remembering so you can tell me what he looks like," Longarm said, his patience shot.

"I don't want any part of trouble," the gunsmith said. "I do a lot of work for them boys."

Longarm's composure snapped for an instant. He jumped inside the shop, grabbed the gunsmith with his left hand, and at the same time drove the heel of his right palm into the stub of the cheap cigar, ramming it deep into the man's throat.

The gunsmith, who had attempted to raise his weapon, suddenly gagged, his eyes bulging and his cheeks blowing outward. Longarm propelled the man backward until he slammed him into a work bench, bending his spine.

"Listen," Longarm said as the man struggled for air with terror flooding his eyes, "I'm in no mood for pleasantries. Now you can swallow that cheap stoggie, suffocate on it, or spit it out, but unless you die, you're going to cooperate. Is that clearly understood?"

The gunsmith nodded. Longarm spun him around, slammed his face down on the bench, and sledgehammered him between the shoulder blades with his closed fist. The cigar appeared, and it took the gunsmith several moments to refill his lungs. By then, his eyes were full of tears and he'd completely lost any remnant of his earlier belligerence.

"A good description of Jack Ramey," Longarm ordered, jerking the man to his toes.

"A drink!" the gunsmith wheezed, pointing to a bottle of whiskey resting beside his bench.

Longarm retrieved the whiskey and allowed the man a drink. The man was very shaken and needed no farther inducement to talk.

"Jack Ramey is short and ugly."

"How short and how ugly?"

"About five-seven with a big, crooked nose and two missing front teeth."

"Upper?"

The gunsmith nodded. "He likes to wear silk bandannas and red is his favorite color."

"How old is the man?"

"About your age."

"Does he pack a hideout?"

"Sure, don't you?"

"I'll ask the questions," Longarm snapped. "Who are his friends?"

"You'll find 'em all at the Champion." The gunsmith's nerve was starting to return and his lip curled with hatred. "And whoever you are, I sure hope they got a big welcoming party waiting for you."

Longarm grabbed the man and bent him back over the work bench. Almost instantly, panic returned to the gunsmith's eyes as he feebly struggled to break Longarm's steely grip.

"I'm a U.S. marshal and I'm going to clean this town up," Longarm told the man. "And when I start sweeping it clean, you're going to be one of the ones that is going out the door. Is that understood?"

"You can't throw me out of Bodie!"

"I can if you're helping to arm my enemies," Longarm told the man in no uncertain terms.

He spun around and continued on his way. People were coming out of their shops and the other saloons to watch him, and Longarm guessed that the best thing he could do was to go into the Champion Saloon fast and low with his gun in his fist.

That's exactly what he did. It wasn't pretty the way he dove in under the swinging bat-wing saloon doors, rolled twice, and came up in a crouch with his gun clenched in

141

his fists. But the welcoming party that awaited his arrival wasn't pretty either.

Someone must have warned Jack Ramey while Longarm had been momentarily detained in the gunsmith's shop, because the room looked empty and the little killer was primed and ready to go to war. He had taken refuge behind the Champion Saloon's long, pine bar, and his first two bullets thundered across the room and ripped apart the swinging bat-wing doors right where Longarm's body should have been.

Longarm's first shot was wide, and the back-bar mirror exploded in a shower of glass. Ramey screamed and dropped behind the bar before Longarm could unleash another bullet. The man popped back into view a few feet away and fired twice more. Longarm's next bullet plugged a case of beer, and foamy brew spewed out of the keg.

"You're under arrest!" Longarm shouted, knocking over a card table and diving behind it for cover. "Throw your gun out and stand up with your hands over your head!"

Ramey didn't answer, but Longarm could hear the killer scuttling over the shattered mirror glass. He heard Ramey knock something over, and then realized that the little gunman was making an escape through the back of the saloon.

"Damn!" Longarm hissed, jumping to his feet.

He was just about to start forward when a sudden movement caught the corner of his eye. Longarm threw himself at the sawdust floor just as the twin barrels of a sawed-off shotgun ripped across the interior of the saloon. Had Longarm been ten more feet away from the blast, its pattern would have shredded him. But he was close enough that the pattern had no time to expand. Unleashing a slug from the muzzle of his revolver into the gut of the bartender was easy.

The bartender, a fat man with muttonchop whiskers, gaped down at Longarm. His smoking shotgun quivered in his fists and his pudgy trigger finger jerked spasmodically.

"It's empty," Longarm explained as he climbed back to his feet and the bartender's glazing eyes rolled up into his forehead. "Sorry."

The bartender pitched forward, impaling himself on his shotgun. He grunted, then rolled off the weapon and crashed facedown into the sawdust.

Longarm darted around the bar and ran almost blindly through a storage room. When he burst out into the alley, he caught a glimpse of Jack Ramey as the man rounded a corner.

Longarm went after the little assassin. He had a good seventy yards to make up, but his legs were much longer than Ramey's and Longarm knew he was a very fast runner. It took him less than ten seconds to reach the corner and when he rounded it, Ramey fired another bullet from across the street.

Longarm saved his remaining bullets. He put his head down and charged across the street. Ramey's next bullet nicked his sleeve, but Longarm didn't even break stride. Ramey turned and vanished between two buildings, running for his life.

Longarm plunged into the dim corridor between the buildings. He thought that Ramey might be out of bullets, but there was always that hideout gun and maybe even another Colt revolver to worry about. As he neared the end of the corridor, Longarm skidded to a halt.

"Ramey!" he shouted, unwilling to burst around another corner and risk getting shot at close range. "You're under arrest! I'm a United States marshal!''

"You're a dead sonofabitch!" Ramey shouted.

Longarm took a deep breath. His lungs were pumping and he batted sawdust from his sweaty face. "Come on out!"

"Go to hell!"

Longarm knew that Ramey wasn't going to surrender. Why should he do that only to face a certain death from the hangman? This one, Longarm knew, was going to be tough.

He crouched low and then removed his hat. Holding it at arm's length, he slipped the edge of its brim around the corner of the building. Ramey took the bait. The distinctive sound of a derringer blanketed the alley. Longarm knew that the derringer might have two shots, but he threw caution to the wind and jumped out into the alley to see Ramey trying to run backward in full retreat.

"Halt!" Longarm shouted.

Ramey fired again, the derringer coughing up its last misspent bullet. Longarm raised his pistol as Jack Ramey turned to run, and when he fired, he shot low. Ramey screamed as Longarm's slug struck him in the back of the thigh. Ramey's leg buckled and he toppled to the dirt, then jumped up and began to hobble toward the next corner.

"Halt!"

When Ramey cursed and kept moving, Longarm coolly shot the man's other leg out from under him. Ramey's scream filled the alley and he collapsed, spitting curses.

Longarm trotted over beside the fallen killer. Ramey was writhing around on his stomach and seemed to be mindless in his pain. But when Longarm grabbed his arm and tried to turn him over, the little gunman had one last card to play and took a vicious swipe at Longarm with a short-bladed pocket knife.

"You're harder to finish than a damned rattlesnake," Longarm grunted, after jumping back with the knee of his pants sliced open.

Ramey tried to lunge at him with the pocket knife and Longarm, having had more than enough from this little assassin, simply booted Ramey in the side of the head. Ramey grunted and his body quivered into stillness.

Longarm searched the man and found that he was carrying almost a thousand dollars cash. "Blood money, I'll bet," Longarm muttered, taking the knife and then the empty derringer and Colt.

He used Ramey's pretty red silk bandanna as a tourniquet on the man's right leg, and Ramey's gunbelt served the same purpose for the left leg. But that didn't completely stop the bleeding.

"I'd like nothing better than to let you bleed to death in this alley on account of what you did to Kane and Ward, but I'm going to make sure that you tell me the whole story and that we get to the bottom of who paid you all this blood money," Longarm told the still figure.

Longarm heard a commotion behind him, and spun around to see men crowded at the entrance to this alleyway. "Hey!" he yelled. "Come give me a hand!"

They hurried forward, and Longarm ordered them to pick Jack Ramey up and carry him over to the jail.

"Don't he need a doctor awful bad first?" a puffing man said as they carried Ramey back to the main street.

"I suppose," Longarm said, noting the condition of Ramey's legs. "Probably at least one of his leg bones is shattered. Dr. Blake is going to hate me for all the work I'm bringing him, but someone had better go find him anyway if he's already left the jail."

As it turned out, Thaddeus Blake had not yet left the jail and the bodies of Marshal Kane and Deputy Ward.

"He the one that shot 'em?" the doctor asked when they carried the unconscious and badly wounded gunman into the jail and laid him on a straw mattress.

"Yeah," Longarm said, "that's Jack Ramey."

"Thought it might be," the doctor said. "He never showed his face much around Bodie. Spent all his time in the Champion Saloon, when he wasn't off raising hell."

"His hellin' days are over," Longarm said. "And so are those of the bartender who works at the Champion."

Blake, who had been about to tear open the pants leg so that he could get at the bullet wounds, looked up suddenly. "You mean you killed *another* one!"

"No," Longarm said, "he was the first man I've killed in Bodie. This little bastard is the one that killed Marshal Kane and his deputy, remember?"

"Yeah," the doctor said. "I just meant . . . well, I just meant that a lot of people have gotten lead poisoning today."

"I know," Longarm said, his mind turning to Megan as he started toward the door, "and a lot more could get the fatal disease before things finally improve."

"Hey!"

Longarm turned at the doorway, suddenly feeling old and tired and in need of a drink. "Yeah?"

"What do we do with Ramey if I can keep him from bleeding to death?"

Longarm thought about that for a moment, then said, "I don't think you have to do anything, Doc. I mean, it's not like he is going to get up and walk out of here."

"No," the doctor said, "but what if someone wants to walk into this office and kill him so that he doesn't talk?"

146

"Good point," Longarm said. "I'm glad someone is still thinking. Doc, if that happens, just excuse yourself and take a walk."

"I will," the doctor assured him.

Longarm nodded, and then he reloaded his gun. The doctor watched him through his bloodshot eyes, and then he shook his head and said, "If you're going to shoot anyone else, don't wound 'em. I'm worn out."

A sardonic smile tugged at the corners of Longarm's mouth. "Doc, I'll sure keep that in mind," he promised as he headed back toward the U.S. Hotel.

Chapter 14

"Darlin', how's the shoulder feeling?" Longarm asked, closing, then locking their hotel room door behind him.

Megan motioned Longarm over to her side, and when he sat down she said, "I heard all the gunshots and I was so afraid that . . ."

Tears started to fill her eyes, and Longarm smiled. "As you can see, I'm just fine."

"What happened?"

"I hunted down, shot the legs out from under, and then arrested a gunman named Jack Ramey." Longarm took a deep breath because the rest was hard to put into words. "Ramey sneaked up behind the jail and gunned Ivan Kane and his deputy."

Megan's hand flew to her mouth and tears filled her eyes. "He *killed them both*!"

"Yeah. Ivan Kane was dying when I got to him, and he identified Ramey as the man who opened fire on them from the cell window. Ramey is well known in Bodie and he wasn't hard to find, but he wasn't in a mood to be arrested."

"But he'll hang, won't he?"

"Damn right he will," Longarm vowed. "If he doesn't die of lead poisoning first. I wasn't the only one that heard that old dying marshal shout Ramey's name."

Megan pulled Longarm down beside her. "I never dreamed that we'd be riding into so much death when we left Reno."

"I told you I thought that things might get pretty rough. I sure wish that you'd never come, Megan. I'll never forgive myself for what happened to your shoulder."

"The shoulder will mend as good as new. And as for the scar, well, you know that it's not my first. There's that one on my butt cheek."

She was smiling, and Longarm remembered that scar where a horse had bit her. "And the little one right up here," he said, patting the soft mound of her breast.

"Yes, the one that you took such great interest in."

Longarm chuckled and stretched out on the bed beside Megan. "I swear that this will all pass and we'll come out of it just fine," he told her. "I think the town is as shocked as we were when it learned about the awful way that Kane and Ward were gunned down while huddled in that jail cell."

"Are people blaming you?"

"I'm sure that some do," Longarm said. "And I have to admit that I'm one of them."

"Don't be," Megan pleaded. "Kane and Ward were out of control. They *were* extorting money from the merchants. Ivan Kane knew he'd corrupted his own reputation."

"Yes," Longarm said, "he knew. And I've seen it happen all too often before. Men like that risk their lives for years and years, and when they begin to get old, slow, and a little afraid, they check their bank accounts and find that they've no savings. Nothing put away and no pension.

At best they get turned out of office with a thank-you by the town council and a few words of gratitude by a bored mayor trying to look good before an election.''

Longarm scowled. "That's why some lawmen go bad at the end of their careers, Megan. They're just finally trying to take care of themselves in their old age.''

"My father hasn't got much in savings, but he never became dishonest.''

"Your father is very special,'' Longarm said.

"Did you ever get that telegram sent off to Denver asking for help?''

"No,'' Longarm answered. "I was going to when all hell broke loose and I never quite got around to it.''

"I think it's still a good idea to send it,'' Megan told him. "You still need help, don't you?''

Longarm dug a cigar out of his vest and found a match, which he ignited on his thumbnail. He rolled off the bed, extracted a bottle of whiskey from his saddlebags, and poured himself a stiff drink.

"You look tired, Custis. You look real tired. Why don't you come to bed with me.''

"Can't. Not yet.''

Megan frowned. "Why not?''

"Because it's still daylight out and I've still got to drag some names out of Jack Ramey. Once I find out who hired him, I'll get to the bottom of things around here.''

"You need some rest and lovin'.''

That made him smile. "Megan, you're *wounded*.''

She smacked her lips. "I'm thirsty. Do you suppose that I could have a little of that whiskey?''

"Hell, yes! Have all you want.''

He poured Megan a glass, and she raised it in a toast and took a long, shuddering gulp. "Now then,'' she said, her voice husky from the drink. "Let's continue with where we left off."

"Megan," he said with a smile, "you are wounded and I'd never touch you for fear of breaking open the wound."

"Hmm," she said, giving the matter and her whiskey some serious contemplation. "Well, I'd respond to that by pointing out to you, Marshal Long, that only one small part of me is wounded. In fact, just a little corner of me. That leaves a whole lot left that is just fine."

"No," he said flatly.

Megan smiled seductively and rolled the bedcover down to her belly. Her breasts were magnificent and despite his low spirits, Longarm felt a stirring inside his pants.

"Do I detect some interest?"

"No, cover up."

Megan took another sip of the whiskey and kicked the bedcovers away. Her long, horsewoman's legs brought a flood of sensual memories back to Longarm, and when she bent her knees and blew him a kiss between her open legs, he simply could stand no more.

"If I so much as cause you a twinge of pain," he said, unbuckling his gunbelt and kicking off his boots, "give me your word that you'll say something."

"I will. I promise I will," she breathed.

"And I'm going to lie sorta off to the side of your belly," he told her as he tore off his shirt and then began to undo his pants. "I'm not going to put any weight on that shoulder and . . ."

"Shut up and mount up," she ordered.

Longarm was big and stiff before he even got his pants off. Megan spread herself wide and moaned with pleasure as he eased into her young body, careful to keep his weight away from that wounded shoulder.

"How's the shoulder?" he whispered after thrusting himself into her fully.

"What shoulder?" she panted, one arm snaking around his neck as he slipped his hand under her firm buttocks and pulled himself even deeper.

Longarm closed his eyes and took her very slowly. He was in no hurry, and he damn sure didn't want to lose control of himself and bang her shoulder and cause it to start hemorrhaging again. Their lovemaking was deep and delicious, and it was nearly twenty minutes before they both started to feel ragged and began to lose control.

A sudden knock at the door froze them. "Marshal? It's Dr. Blake."

Longarm groaned into the small of Megan's moist neck. She clutched him even tighter and whispered, "Custis, ignore him. Please!"

Longarm thought that was a wonderful idea. He began his slow but hard pumping again, feeling a tingling sensation spreading all the way from the roots of his hair to the tips of his toes.

"Marshal Long!"

They both heard the door handle as the doctor turned it one way and then the next. "Marshal, unlock this door!"

"Later!" Longarm yelled, raising his head. "Come back in fifteen minutes."

"No, a half hour!" Megan gasped.

"Oh for crying out loud!" Blake bellowed. "She's half dead! Are you both crazy!"

"Go away!" Longarm grunted. "She ain't dead yet!"

The doctor gave them a good cussing, but neither Longarm or Megan heard him because they were both moaning and thrusting, each lost in his or her explosion of sweet passion.

153

"You ought to be ashamed of yourself," Dr. Blake said later when Longarm went downstairs to the lobby and summoned him back upstairs. "Good God, man, have you lost your senses!"

"For a while we both did," Longarm admitted.

"Marshal Long, do you realize how much blood she lost and what would happen if that shoulder opened up again!" Blake was actually furious, as Longarm knew he had every right to be.

"We were very, very careful," Longarm explained.

"Careful isn't good enough," the doctor barked as he went into their hotel room, fire in his eyes and whiskey in his gut. "Young woman, if this... this monster has..."

"It was all my idea," Megan said, looking more amused than ashamed. "I seduced him, not the other way around."

"You're not very responsible, and you're certainly in no physical condition to be doing that."

"Doctor, I really think you had better stick to things medical," Megan told him, her smile fading. "Custis makes me feel better."

Blake looked as if he were going to have a fit. Instead, he clamped his mouth shut, sat down on the bed, and rolled back the blanket to study his bandage.

"Well?" Megan asked.

"It doesn't appear to have reopened," the doctor said after peeling back some tape so that he could lift the bandage up and examine the wound itself. "And I'd say that was a wonder."

"We do wonderful things when we are both in bed," Megan said happily.

"Megan!" Longarm snapped, trying hard to look stern.

"How is the pain?" Blake asked.

"It's manageable."

"I can smell whiskey on your breath."

"I can smell whiskey on your breath too," Megan said. "You're such a good doctor that I wish you didn't drink so much."

"No lectures."

"Why *do* you drink so much, Dr. Blake?"

"I drink too much because I've seen far too much death and carnage," he said, opening his medical kit and reaching for some pills. "Take these for pain instead of whiskey. All right?"

"All right."

Dr. Blake stood up. "I'll be back tomorrow morning, and I'll expect you to have enjoyed a very good night's sleep."

He shot a withering glance at Longarm. "Is that clearly understood by the both of you?"

"Yes, sir," Longarm said.

"Yes, Doctor," Megan replied.

"Doc?" Longarm asked.

"What?"

"If you're leaving, would you deliver a message to the next stage headed for Carson City? I have to get a telegram sent to Denver to let them know what is going on here."

"And asking them to send immediate assistance, I hope."

"Yeah," Longarm said. "That too."

"All right. Write the message out and I'll see that it leaves on the next stage bound for Carson City."

Longarm quickly scribbled a note. He dug into his pockets and found three dollars. "Doc, tell the stagecoach driver or whoever it is that will deliver this message that

I need a quick reply and I'll pay him another three dollars if I get it back by tomorrow night."

"All right."

Dr. Blake took the message and the crumpled bills and shoved them into his pocket. Before leaving, he actually wagged a bony forefinger at Megan and Longarm saying, "A good night's sleep, is that clear?"

"Couldn't be clearer," Longarm said. "And stop worrying. I'm going to have to spend the night camped next to Jack Ramey."

"That won't be necessary."

Longarm's jaw dropped. "Why not?"

"The bullet that hit his right leg severed an artery. I just couldn't get it tied off in time. Ramey went into shock and died of blood loss."

Longarm's hand brushed across his eyes. "I'm sorry," he said. "Thanks for trying, Doc. I thought Ramey was going to be the key that would unlock everything. I thought he was going to give me names, facts, and figures."

"Maybe he already did."

Longarm blinked. "I don't understand."

"Men often confess their deepest secrets when they're told by a doctor that there is no hope."

"Not men like Jack Ramey. He was a snake."

"Even snakes love their children."

Longarm took a step toward the doctor. "Don't dance around with me, Doc. What are you trying to say?"

"I'm saying that Jack Ramey had, as you well know, almost a thousand dollars cash. He also had a five-year-old illegitimate son that lives in Santa Fe. He gave me the kid's name and—"

Longarm was suddenly so excited that he interrupted. "And in exchange for that name and the promise to see

156

that his kid got the thousand dollars, he told you something.''

"Exactly.''

"Who hired him?''

The doctor was wearing a battered derby hat. He smiled and tipped it to them. "If you're good little boys and girls tonight,'' he said, "and if I can see that that young lady has had a full and restful night's sleep, then tomorrow morning when I come by again, I'll be happy to tell you what Jack Ramey told me.''

"You can't do that! It's obstruction of justice!''

"It's obstruction of something,'' the doctor said coolly as his eyes flicked to Longarm's crotch for just a fraction of a second, "but it's hardly justice.''

"Damn!'' Longarm swore as the door banged shut in his face.

Megan took the blackmail more in stride. "It's only six o'clock,'' she said. "We've got hours before it's time to go to sleep, don't we?''

"Yes, but I hate someone holding something over me,'' Longarm groused. "It's the principle of the thing, Megan.''

"I agree,'' she said, "but what can we do other than make the best of the next few hours together?''

Longarm could see the practical wisdom of her words. And with that thought in mind, he bolted the door again, then undressed and climbed back into bed with Megan.

Chapter 15

When the doctor called the next morning, Longarm and
Megan were fully dressed and just finishing a huge breakfast that they had ordered to be delivered to their room.

"Well, well," the doctor said, surveying the room and
the fresh-faced couple with approval. "You look very
much more rested this morning."

"And you look fit this morning yourself," Longarm
said, noting how the doctor's eyes were clearer and his
face less puffy from the heavy drinking.

"Good, then," the doctor said, coming over to sit beside Megan. "I'll change the bandages now and apply
some more medicinal ointments."

He placed his hand on Megan's brow. "No fever,
which is an excellent sign that you are already on the
mend."

"I feel much better today," Megan said. She winked
at Longarm and added, "We got a very good night's
sleep."

"So it would appear," the doctor mumbled as he removed the bandages and studied the bullet wound. "You
know, there are gifted surgeons in San Francisco who

could reduce the scarring and . . ."

"It's all right," Megan said. "Custis isn't interested in my shoulder anyway, are you, Custis?"

Longarm blushed. Megan, he knew, was being wicked, and even a mild castigation would only provoke her to become even more outrageous.

"Custis likes the rest of me just fine."

"That's enough," Longarm warned, the tips of his mustache twitching with irritation.

Dr. Blake's examination and ministrations took only a few minutes. Satisfied that the wound was healing nicely, he finished his rebandaging and then closed his medical kit in preparation to leaving.

"Did you get my message off by stage last evening?" Longarm asked.

"I did. It ought to reach Carson City this afternoon and then be sent very soon afterward."

"Good."

Longarm looked at Megan. "I took the liberty of adding a message to be telegraphed to your father in Reno. I didn't want him to be worried."

"Did you tell him about my . . . accident?"

"No," Longarm said. "I thought it better not to."

Megan looked relieved.

"And now," Longarm said, turning to face Dr. Blake. "We've kept our promise, so it's time to keep yours. What did Jack Ramey say yesterday before bleeding to death?"

The doctor frowned, and then moved over to the window. "Are you sure that you want to know? That it wouldn't just be better to go back to Reno and put this hellhole named Bodie behind you?"

"I'm *very* sure," Longarm said without hesitation. "Because if I did that, I'd be allowing whoever paid Jack

Ramey to get away scot-free. They'd probably continue to hire men to do their butchery so that anytime someone tried to stand up for the law in this town, they'd be assassinated just like Hec and Ivan.''

''Yes,'' the doctor said, ''that's quite likely. But once I tell you who hired Ramey, you'll feel duty-bound to open that can of worms and then there will be even more bloodshed. And frankly, Marshal Long, even Bodie has seen enough for a while.''

''Doc, I appreciate your concern, but I've got a job to do. Now, I know that Marshal Kane and his deputy weren't even authorized to carry badges. They told me that.''

''That surprises me.''

''It shouldn't,'' Longarm said. ''I'd have found out quick enough. And I also know that they were shaking down some of the merchants.''

''And some of the professionals,'' the doctor admitted with a trace of bitterness. ''Their protection fees were not exorbitant, considering the alternatives. And quite frankly, those who were convinced that it was better to subscribe are, in the main, satisfied with the protection that they were receiving.''

''Receiving from whom?''

''From a coalition of powerful men, Marshal. I would say they number less than five. They are the most powerful among our saloon owners and mine owners, and one is a miners' union boss.''

''What has a miners' union boss got to do with this sort of thing?'' Megan asked.

The doctor shrugged. ''Greed knows no occupational boundaries, dear girl. The miners' union is powerful here in Bodie, and its president wants a say-so in every facet of Bodie's day-to-day activities.''

"Did he also want to see Marshal Kane and Deputy Ward killed?"

"Probably," the doctor said, "but not enough to pay someone to do the job."

"Then who the hell *did* pay Jack Ramey!" Longarm demanded with no small amount of exasperation.

"The name that Ramey gave me is that of Horace Leach."

"Horace Leach?" Longarm said, turning the name over in his mind and coming up with a blank. "Who the hell is he?"

"He is a very private man who owns the Savior Mining Company. The property is located about three miles east of Bodie. Mr. Leach is a certified mining engineer, and he did quite well on the Comstock Lode before his presence became a burden and he was forced to relocate. He bought one of Bodie's oldest mines, one thought to be worked out several years ago. But Mr. Leach's geological education paid off handsomely, and he soon resurrected its productive capacity. I would say that the Savior Mine now produces about half a million dollars of gold and silver a year. That's nothing compared to the Standard Mine, which is our largest, but it's not anything to sniff at either."

"I should say not," Longarm replied. "So why did Mr. Leach hate Kane and Ward bad enough to pay an assassin?"

"They had a run-in, of course. It happened last fall. Mr. Leach is known for throwing these huge extravagant parties for his stockholders and potential stockholders. From what I'd heard, the two men had never liked each other, and things got much worse when Marshal Kane offered his services to 'protect' the guests that were coming to Bodie to enjoy Leach's grand party."

"I see," Longarm said. "So the marshal wanted to extort a little protection for Mr. Leach's guests?"

"Exactly!" the doctor said. "I'm sure that Ivan thought it would bring him at least several thousand dollars. Mr. Leach, however, had other ideas. He believed that he had enough power and influence that his guests would be well protected."

"I take it that Mr. Leach has his own gunnies?"

"A few," the doctor said. "They come and they go. Right now he has about three on his staff. They guard the ore shipments as well as his other interests and his person. They are a very ruthless bunch, that I can assure you. They have provided me with a fair amount of business."

"I see."

"Why didn't Mr. Leach use one of his own men instead of Jack Ramey?" Megan asked.

"Good question," the doctor replied, "and one that I also asked myself. The best answer I can figure is that it was cleaner to hire a cold-blooded little executioner like Jack Ramey. A man who would gun down the marshal and the deputy and then disappear never to return."

"Ramey's fatal mistake," Longarm said, "was to delay his departure."

"I can assure you, Marshal Long, that Jack Ramey was not known for his caution or his brilliance. His cronies and bedfellows practically lived at the Champion Saloon. They were so egregious that they drove out any respectable clients and had it all to themselves."

"Egregious?"

"It means someone or something that is remarkably bad." Dr. Blake shook his head. "And believe me, Jack Ramey and his fellow lowlifes who had taken over the Champion Saloon were the worst of Bodie's worst."

"I see."

163

"Anyway," the doctor continued, "Horace Leach is the man who paid Jack Ramey a thousand dollars to execute those murders."

"How do I get to the man without dying for my trouble?" Longarm asked.

"I don't really know," the doctor replied. "I can tell you this. Horace Leach is a very intelligent and prudent man. If he even suspects that we know he is the one behind those jail-cell murders, we are all as good as dead."

"And I suppose," Longarm said, "that the Savior Mine and its surrounding property are a veritable fortress?"

"Of course. There are armed guards everywhere. He has a large house on the property and three gunmen live downstairs. I've heard that one of them is always on guard. They do not drink when on duty, and they are not allowed to bring any women on the premises that might distract them."

"What about his mining crews?" Longarm asked.

"What about them?"

"Are they loyal?"

"Not particularly," the doctor decided after a moment's reflection. "Leach has a very poor reputation as an employer. He'll fire anyone who gets hurt in a mining accident, and the Savior is always the lowest-paying among the big mines. Furthermore, Leach has an abominable reputation for safety on the jobs. His mines are the most dangerous by far. I'm told he cuts every corner possible, even trying to save money by inadequately shoring up his shafts and tunnels."

"He sounds like a real skunk," Megan said.

"He's not a nice man," the doctor agreed. "I've attended two of the soiled doves who frequent the Leach Mansion, and both were suffering from severe beatings and some rather hideous sexual perversions."

164

When Longarm saw Megan's eyebrows shoot up with curiosity, he growled, "Never mind, Megan!"

The doctor seconded that by saying, "My dear, you most certainly would not enjoy hearing the things that Leach does to women. It would be neither enlightening nor pleasant to contemplate."

"All right," Megan said. "So don't tell me what he does to them. Dr. Blake, why don't you just tell us how we stop this terrible man?"

Longarm whirled toward Megan. "There is no *we* in this matter," he said very firmly. "You're in no shape at all to leave your sickbed."

"Custis, you of all people know that I'm still in pretty good shape."

"Stay in bed and keep the door locked and a gun by your side," Longarm ordered. "Megan, I have to bring down Horace Leach alone, and I sure don't want to be worrying about you. Or you either, Doctor."

Blake smiled wanly. "I sincerely appreciate your concern. But I think that I am quite safe because I am entirely unworthy of one of Mr. Leach's paid assassins."

He snapped his bag closed and went to the door. "I wish that I could say the same for the both of you. I wish that you had just taken my advice and left Bodie forever."

"Thank you," Megan said. "Will you be returning soon?"

"Tomorrow," the doctor said as he turned to go. "That is, God willing."

When they were alone again, Longarm bolted the door and went over to Megan. He took her hands in his own and said, "I'm going after Horace Leach tonight and I can't be worrying about you, Megan."

"I'll keep my door bolted and a gun at my side."

"Not good enough," Longarm told her. "I want to relocate you tonight."

"To where?"

"Another room in another hotel. Somewhere that they wouldn't be able to find you in case things do not go quite as well as planned."

Megan squeezed his hand. "You mean in case you are killed trying to arrest Horace Leach?"

There was no sense in lying to the young woman, so Longarm just nodded his head. "Something like that, yes. And if I was absolutely sure that your shoulder could stand the bumps and jolts of traveling back to Reno, I'd put you on the evening stagecoach."

"I wouldn't go," she told him. "I'd never leave without knowing that you were all right."

Longarm gently took her in his arms. "I ought to go and get ready for tonight," he whispered as she slid her hand between the buttons of his shirt and began to rub his chest. "I ought to go now."

"No," she breathed, her breath hot in his ear. "You need to make love to me all day long."

Longarm smiled, and decided that there really wasn't much in the way of preparations that he could undertake anyway other than relocating Megan to another hotel and room.

"I suppose that we can wait a few hours before we sneak you out the back way and find another hotel."

"At least a few hours," she said, reaching for him.

"All right," he said, cupping her breast and then bringing it to his mouth. "We might as well enjoy what time we may have left."

Megan closed her eyes and let the waves of pleasure sweep over her as she whispered, "Darling, I couldn't agree more."

Chapter 16

Longarm relocated Megan to the Grand Central Hotel, which was located on Main Street just below the King Street intersection and across from Wagner's Saloon. It had a reputation for being an establishment of quality and Longarm knew that the owner, George Summers, and his manager, S.N. Pitcher, were very proud of their elegant banquet facilities and the twenty-one luxuriously furnished rooms upstairs, every one of which boasted its own window.

"This place even has its own indoor plumbing," Longarm said when he had Megan comfortably resting in her new room with its elegant chandelier and brocaded velvet wallpaper.

"Its own plumbing?"

"Sure," Longarm said, going over to turn on a facet. "Mr. Summers had a well dug at the back of the property along with a large pump that forces water up into all the rooms."

"Is it hot for bathing?"

"No," Longarm said, "but they'll bring you up hot water."

Megan looked around. "This is really nice," she said. "Why didn't we come here first?"

"This room costs two dollars a night," Longarm told her.

Megan patted the bed. "It's only a single. We need a bigger one."

"This will do for tonight," he told her. "Tomorrow, after I've taken care of Leach, we can see about moving to a larger suite."

Longarm went to the window and watched the sun fade into the Sierra peaks. "I had better be on my way," he told her. "I've got some preparations to make."

"Come over here and hold me," Megan said. "I'm afraid for you, Custis."

He went over to hold the girl. "Don't be," he said, trying to ease her worries. "I'm an old hand at this sort of thing. My plan is to go in about midnight, sneak past Leach's gunnies, and take him by surprise in his bed."

"But then he'll sound the alarm and you'll be surrounded!" Megan wailed. "Custis, I don't think that is any kind of a plan at all."

"I haven't told you all of it," he said. "Once I get to Leach, I'll make sure that he can't sound the alarm. I'll knock him out, toss him over my shoulder, and sneak off the Savior Mine's property. I'll have Horace Leach in custody and behind bars by three o'clock tomorrow morning."

"But even if you can do all that," Megan argued, her voice strained with apprehension, "don't you see that his friends are likely to come for him? Those gunnies want to keep getting paid. Custis, they won't rest until they free Leach and put an end to you."

Longarm frowned. In truth, he had been afraid of the same thing. If Ivan Kane and his deputy had still been

168

alive, they would probably have supported him. But with them gone, Megan and Dr. Blake were his only remaining allies, and they could not be counted on to provide much help.

Hell, he wouldn't even allow them to help.

"Why don't you do this," Megan suggested. "Get my horses saddled and ready the ones we rode down here as well as the ones that I bought, and let's make a run for Carson City. Once there, no one would dare touch us and you'll have all the help you need."

"It's not a bad plan," Longarm said, "except that you can't travel with that shoulder."

"But I *can* travel!"

"Not on horseback."

Megan was nearly beside herself. "Then . . . then let's buy or borrow or even *steal* a buggy or wagon! Custis, you haven't a prayer in Bodie! Can't you see that?"

Longarm stood up and began to pace back and forth, hands clasped behind his back, mind working furiously. He knew in his heart that Megan was right because, even if he did get Horace Leach out of his mansion, he'd never be able to hold off all of Leach's friends, which would probably include part of that coalition that held Bodie in its firm control.

"All right," he said. "I'll line up a wagon and figure out a way for us to make a run for it tonight. Maybe by the time that people around here realize we're gone, we'll have too big a head start for them to catch up with us."

"Now you're talking!" Megan said with a big grin of relief. "So we won't even be using this room tonight?"

"I guess not."

"It would be a shame," Megan said, eyes dancing, "not to at least enjoy ourselves here in this beautiful room."

"No," Longarm said flatly. "Absolutely not!"

"Oh," she pouted. "Are you sure?"

Longarm wasn't sure of anything when it came to this passionate young woman. So he headed for the door before his body overruled his brain.

"Good-bye," he said at the door.

"I'm not sure that I'm going to be able to lie here waiting and wondering if you are alive or dead, Custis."

"I'm afraid," he told her, "that you have no choice."

"I'll be ready," she called as the door softly closed behind him. "I'll be ready to run away with you!"

Longarm went to the Kirkwood Livery Stable. Megan trusted Kirkwood, and Longarm figured the man would not betray him.

"So," Kirkwood said, toeing the earth and looking skeptical as hell, "you're fixin' to kidnap Horace Leach and deliver him to justice in Carson City."

"That's the plan."

"Well," Kirkwood said, spitting a stream of tobacco into the dirt and then wiping his lips with the back of his sleeve, "all I got to say is that you better be both good and lucky."

"I am pretty good at what I do," Longarm said. "But I try not to count on luck."

"You're going to have to have a lot of luck to pull this one off," Kirkwood opinioned. " 'Cause, even if you do somehow manage to get Leach out of his house, they'll come swarmin' after you like a cloud of hornets. Ain't no wagon gonna get you far enough ahead of 'em."

Longarm frowned. "Maybe I can lose them," he said. "There's a lot of wagon tracks on the road to Carson."

"Yeah," Kirkwood agreed. "There is. But everyone they meet comin' south will have seen you. Marshal, you can be damn sure that Leach's boys and them others that are all tied up together under the saloon owners and union and such are going to be asking a lot of questions of passerbys. They'll know how far a lead you got on 'em and they'll make it up.''

"You're saying I'll definitely be overtaken?''

"Hell, yes! It's well over a hundred miles to Carson City. Ain't no way you can get a big enough jump on them boys to reach the capital without being run down and killed.''

Longarm was plenty willing to fend for himself, but the idea of having Megan also overtaken and killed was more than he could bear to think about.

"I got a suggestion," Kirkwood said.

Longarm's head snapped up. "I'm all ears.''

"Give me them sorrels that you rode into town on and I'll hide you, Miss Riley, and old Horace Leach hisself in a supply wagon and deliver you safely to Carson City.''

Hope sprang up in Longarm. "You could do that?''

"I take horses, hay, and supplies to Carson City quite regularly," the liveryman said. "Wouldn't be anything out of the ordinary. And I always carry a big double-barreled shotgun for protection. I had to kill a couple highwaymen about two years ago and it wasn't pretty. People don't fart around with me when I'm on that wagon with my shotgun.''

"It just might work," Longarm agreed.

"It *will* work, Marshal Long. 'Cause, if it don't, I'll be as dead as you and Miss Riley, and I don't much cotton to that notion.''

"Okay," Longarm said, "we'll give it a try.''

"But I want her matched sorrels," Kirkwood repeated.

"I'm sure that, given the circumstances, Miss Riley will agree to that.''

"You better ask her first."

"I will," Longarm said vaguely. He wasn't about to get into an argument with Megan over the sorrels. She'd be adamantly opposed to giving them over, of course. But they were fair compensation for the price of their lives.

"Then we got a deal. Bring Leach and the girl around tonight and I'll have everything ready."

"Won't they think it odd that you left in the middle of the night?"

"Nope," Kirkwood said, " 'cause I do it sometimes to escape the heat and all the road traffic. Anyway, I do sell hay and such things as I can peddle along the road, and I can always say that I left this evening in order to make a sale."

"You've got all the answers, haven't you, Mr. Kirkwood."

"Not all of 'em," the livery man said. "But I damn sure better have 'em come tomorrow when them Leach gunnies and the others catch up with me. Otherwise . . ."

Kirkwood did not finish his sentence, but instead drew a long, dirty forefinger across his gullet, and that made his meaning plenty clear enough.

Shortly before midnight, Longarm tied his horse in an arroyo just a quarter of a mile north of the Savior Mine and its many large outbuildings. He briefly considered bringing a rifle with him, but then discarded the idea because he wasn't going to be able to carry an unconscious Horace Leach and a rifle. No, he'd have to rely on his side arms.

"Just don't start to whinnying," he warned the sorrel gelding. "I'll be back within an hour, I hope."

Longarm's single advantage was that the moon was only a thin wedge of light and the night was very dark.

There were even clouds in the sky to hide an otherwise brilliant field of stars. The Savior Mine was shut down for the night, and almost all the lights were extinguished.

Giving the sorrel one last friendly pat, Longarm struck across the sage-covered ground moving low but as fast as possible. His only immediate fear was dogs, but he doubted they would sound any alarm or warning since there were so many men coming and going on these premises. Longarm used one of the mansion's lit upstairs windows as his beacon. Longarm figured that the upstairs room might well be where Horace Leach slept or fornicated with the prostitutes for which he apparently had such a large appetite.

Fifteen minutes later, Longarm was gliding across the mansion's wide front porch and slipping through the front door. It didn't even have a lock since Leach had three guards living in the mansion for protection. And Longarm, remembering that one of them was always supposed to be on alert, moved very quietly. His thinking was that, if he could find that single waking guard and put him out of commission until morning, he would have an excellent chance of abducting Horace Leach without any fuss or interference.

The night guard was sitting at a small table in the kitchen with a cup of coffee. His back was to Longarm as he read the *Standard*, Bodie's thrice-weekly newspaper. Tiptoeing forward, Longarm silently drew his pistol, then laid a deep crease in the guard's scalp.

The man pitched forward, striking his forehead on the edge of the table. His coffee cup spilled from his hand and shattered on the floor, raising quite a racket.

Longarm grabbed the unconscious guard's collar. He thought he heard someone call from upstairs as he dragged the guard into a pantry and shut the door behind him. Longarm paused, listening. When he was sure that no one was coming, Longarm cleaned up the mess, disposed of it so no one would be suspicious for a while, and then headed upstairs to retrieve Horace Leach. Time, Longarm knew, was of the essence. Every minute's head start that he could gain on Leach's gunnies and anyone else who would be following would be to his great advantage.

"All right," Longarm whispered as he mounted the stairs hearing a woman giggling and then a man's raw laughter. "Here we go."

Chapter 17

When Longarm pushed Horace Leach's bedroom door open, he was not prepared for the scene that he saw. Leach was vigorously riding one prostitute while his face was buried in the crotch of a second who was standing straddle-legged on top of his bed. They were in such a frenzy of passion that none of them even noticed Longarm until he walked right up to the bed and jammed the barrel of his six-gun into Leach's bony ribs.

"Party is over for tonight," Longarm said, cocking his gun so there could be no doubt about his intentions. "So get your face out of her bush and all three of you climb off the bed."

Leach was a man in his early sixties, tall, thin, and with a little potbelly. He wasn't much of a figure of manhood either as he twisted around to gape at Longarm.

"Who . . ."

Longarm jolted Leach with a short but powerful left cross. The mine owner toppled over sideways and one of the prostitutes started to scream, but Longarm poked her in the fanny with the barrel of his Colt, saying, "You don't want to make a sound or it could be fatal for all of us. Do you understand?"

The woman, a fat, buxom blonde, nodded her double chins. She was well past her prime. The other was dark-complected and coarse-looking, with several missing teeth. Leach had a lot more money than taste, Longarm decided.

"You women just get dressed. If you keep your mouths shut, we might all survive this evening."

"Who are you!" the dark one demanded.

"I'm the one doing all the talking here, remember?"

The woman gulped. She was tough as a dried cowhide and not a bit afraid, but she was also smart enough to read a man and know when he wasn't bluffing.

Leach was groaning and holding the side of his rapidly swelling jaw. His nearly hairless body was bathed in perspiration and his potbelly was heaving as if he'd run several miles. He disgusted Longarm, adding to the hatred Longarm already felt toward the mine owner for killing Kane and Ward.

"Get dressed, Horace. We're going for a long ride."

The man tried to protest, but instead moaned piteously.

"I guess I broke your jaw," Longarm said. "Too bad. Now, if you don't want your *neck* broken as well, I suggest you just do as I say and no one will get hurt. Hell, we might even live to tell our friends about what happened tonight."

"What about us?" the fat one demanded to know as she and her friend dressed.

"Well, you are a problem," Longarm admitted. "I don't suppose that I could trust you to just leave this place and keep your mouths shut for about twelve hours."

The woman's hateful expression told Longarm that he couldn't trust her to keep her mouth shut even twelve seconds.

"In that case," Longarm said, "we'll just have to tie

you both up and leave it at that."

"You ain't tyin' me up," the woman hissed.

Longarm had a knife, and now he brought it out. "I think you'd rather be tied up with a gag in your big mouth than have your throat slit, wouldn't you?"

The woman paled, and Longarm was greatly relieved to see that his bluff had accomplished its purpose. Keeping an eye on the moaning Horace Leach, he quickly bound the two prostitutes up, hog-tying them naked.

"I hope the fellas that find you ladies tomorrow morning are gentlemen," Longarm said with a devilish wink. When the dark one cursed him, Longarm filled her mouth with her own dirty underwear. "Now you," he said to the blonde.

She shook her head, and Longarm was forced to bend her head back, pry open her jaws, and fill her mouth before binding it shut.

"I'm sorry you ladies are going to spend the rest of the night in such an uncomfortable and unladylike position," he said. "But at least you'll get through this alive, which might be more than either I or Mr. Leach here can predict with any certainty."

Leach had been using opium, and Longarm could smell its sweetish smoke in the room. That was fine with him. A man doped up on opium was always far more passive than one who was boozed up and infused with whiskey courage.

"Get dressed," Longarm ordered.

Leach fumbled with a bathrobe and then his slippers. Longarm had a decision to make, and that was whether to knock Leach unconscious and carry him to the waiting sorrel, or try to march the murdering bastard out of the house and across the sagebrush.

Longarm decided that he could not trust Leach to keep

quiet, so he walked over to the man and said, "I'm sorry about breaking your damn jaw but I got to add insult to injury."

He pistol-whipped Horace Leach across the side of the head. It wasn't something that gave Longarm any satisfaction despite the knowledge of what this man done to Kane and Ward. Leach's knobby knees buckled and he collapsed. Longarm picked him up, tossed the man over his left shoulder, and went back downstairs.

Twenty minutes later Leach was getting real heavy, but now the horse could carry the half-naked mine owner.

"Thank God, you made it!" Megan cried, throwing herself into Longarm's embrace and hugging him with her one good arm as tightly as possible.

"So far," Longarm said, "so good."

He glanced over at Kirkwood. "Everything ready?"

Kirkwood nodded. He showed them a modified freight wagon loaded with sacks of grain and a pile of grass hay. The wagon had sides about three feet tall and it looked ready to fall apart, but Longarm was sure that Kirkwood had a lot of faith in the vehicle or he would not have used it at such an important time as this.

"Let's go," Kirkwood said, eyeing the mine owner with contempt. "Marshal, I still think you should have put Leach out of his misery back at the mine."

"I want him to confess to the authorities in Carson City," Longarm said by way of a quick explanation. "After he does, I think we can get some tough but honest lawmen down here to make some permanent changes for Bodie."

"Now that," Kirkwood said, "would be great. Load up!"

Longarm helped Megan into the wagon and covered her

with hay. Then he tossed Horace Leach up, but not before he gagged the man. "Cover him well," he said to Megan.

"What about you?"

"I'll ride up with Kirkwood at least until sunrise."

The liveryman nodded his approval, and then he took his seat and slapped his lines to the rumps of their horses.

"You tell Miss Riley about them sorrel horses?" Kirkwood asked as they headed north along the dim and almost empty main street of Bodie.

"Yeah," Longarm lied, unwilling to jeopardize this man's cooperation for the time being.

"Good. I'm glad to see that she has that much good sense," Kirkwood said with satisfaction as they left the town and hurried into what would be a long, dark night.

When dawn finally sneaked over the eastern horizon some five hours later, they were still moving at a good clip.

"Say, Custis," Megan called, "when can we come back to get all my horses?"

Kirkwood looked sideways at him and Longarm spluttered, "Soon."

"They ain't all your horses anymore," Kirkwood declared. "The sorrels are mine now."

Megan popped up from under the hay. "What?"

"You agreed to give 'em to me in exchange for me risking my neck."

"I did no such thing!"

Kirkwood drew the wagon to a sudden stop. "All right," he said, "both of you get the hell off this wagon and take Leach with you."

"No," Longarm said, eyes going to Megan. "Please, be reasonable."

"I'm not giving him my sorrels! And I paid him for two other horses."

179

"You can have 'em," Kirkwood said. "That palomino *is* wind-broke. Knew it all along, and the other is too small for a man. So take 'em—but I keep the sorrels."

"No!" Megan shouted.

"Get down," Kirkwood said, grabbing up his shotgun. "Our deal is off."

"Now wait a minute," Longarm said, almost pleading. "Megan, they are *just horses.*"

"They're a lot more than that to me!"

"Are they worth more than our lives? Than bringing Horace Leach and his ruthless friends to justice? Than avenging the slaughter of Ivan Kane and Hec Ward?"

Megan finally got hold of her senses and said, "No, I guess not."

"All right then," Longarm said with genuine relief. "This is done. Let's stop haggling and go on!"

Kirkwood was petulant, but he very much wanted the sorrels so he drove on. They passed other wagons all morning, and almost all of them knew Kirkwood and hailed him as they passed, heading for Bodie.

"Here comes the stagecoach," Kirkwood said about noon. He pulled his pocket watch from his vest. "And it's right on time."

Kirkwood waved to the coach, and Longarm did too. It passed in a great cloud of dust, and they would have thought no more of it except the thing turned around and quickly overtook them.

"What the hell!" Kirkwood shouted as the stage driver drew up alongside, almost running them off the road.

Longarm had only to look up at the stage driver and the man sitting beside him to understand what had made the stage turn around.

"You sonofabitch!" Wild Bill Riley shouted. "Where the hell is my daughter!"

Megan, upon hearing her father's voice, popped out from under the hay and cried, "Father!"

When Wild Bill saw the bandage covering Megan's wounded shoulder, he almost shot Longarm. It took quite some time to calm him down, and he might still have shot Longarm if they hadn't convinced him that all of their lives were in danger.

"If they're coming after us, let's make a stand," Wild Bill shouted, recklessly waving his gun.

Longarm gave the matter some consideration. He turned to Kirkwood. "I suppose you'll want to leave."

"Yep. You'll all get killed."

After ten minutes of strenuous debate, Kirkwood was talked into handing over his team of horses and the wagon. He would take the stagecoach back to Bodie, then pick them up in Carson City, where Longarm was to deliver them to a friend.

"Good luck!" he shouted.

As it turned out, they didn't need luck until they were almost to the Mormon settlement of Genoa. By then, they could almost see the outskirts of Carson City.

"There's only four of them," Longarm said, looking back at their pursuers from Bodie. "We can handle that many among ourselves."

Wild Bill was all for stopping or even turning around and charging the four onrushing riders. Longarm, however, was much more practical. He simply topped a low ridge and then drove down a little ways before setting the brake.

"They can't see the wagon," he told Megan and her father. "So we'll just hike back up to the crest of the hill and catch 'em by surprise."

They were waiting and ready when the four hired gunmen from Bodie came thundering up the rise. Longarm jumped up and shouted, "You're all under arrest!"

The horsemen, caught completely by surprise, drew their guns. Wild Bill emptied his gun first, but because of his eyes, hit nothing. Longarm got three of the riders, the last one nearly running him down.

Megan proved her worth and her marksmanship by emptying a fourth saddle.

"I got 'em!" Wild Bill whooped as he squinted into the late afternoon sunshine at the riderless horses which had turned and were galloping back toward Bodie. "I got at least three of the four, didn't I!"

"Yes," Longarm said, winking at Megan. "You did."

"And my girl," Wild Bill said, "she got the fourth."

Longarm didn't hesitate. "That's right."

Wild Bill grinned and heaved a sigh of contentment. "I guess we did it then, huh."

"We sure did, Father."

The old tail-twister reloaded and then he squinted at Longarm. "Did you diddle my daughter in Bodie, Marshal?"

"I . . ."

"If you did, I'm going to shoot your goddamn balls off soon as I get my gun reloaded," Wild Bill vowed, fumbling at his cartridge belt for reloads.

"He did not," Megan said, stepping between the two men. "Father, he took very good care of me."

"He let you get shot!"

"But he also saved my life, and now he's going to see that Bodie is cleaned up forever."

"Oh, yeah?" the old man challenged.

"Yeah," Longarm said.

"How you gonna do that?"

Longarm walked over to the wagon and dragged the now-conscious Horace Leach out from under the hay. The

182

man's face was as round as a mellon. He looked pitiful.

"This is the man that had your old friend Marshal Ivan Kane murdered as well as his deputy."

Wild Bill forgot about his threat against Longarm, and hurried to reload his pistol all the while muttering over and over, "Then I'll shoot *his* balls off!"

Longarm guessed, if worse came to worst and he could not save Leach's balls, that wouldn't be such an all-fired tragedy anyway.

Watch for

LONGARM AND THE SHIVAREE RIDERS

202nd in the bold LONGARM series
from Jove

Coming in October!

If you enjoyed this book, subscribe now and get...

TWO FREE

A $7.00 VALUE–

If you would like to read more of the very best, most exciting, adventurous, action-packed Westerns being published today, you'll want to subscribe to True Value's Western Home Subscription Service.

Each month the editors of True Value will select the 6 very best Westerns from America's leading publishers for special readers like you. You'll be able to preview these new titles as soon as they are published, *FREE* for ten days with no obligation!

TWO FREE BOOKS

When you subscribe, we'll send you your first month's shipment of the newest and best 6 Westerns for you to preview. With your first shipment, two of these books will be yours as our introductory gift to you absolutely *FREE* (a $7.00 value), regardless of what you decide to do. If

you like them, as much as we think you will, keep all six books but pay for just 4 at the low subscriber rate of just $2.75 each. If you decide to return them, keep 2 of the titles as our gift. No obligation.

Special Subscriber Savings

When you become a True Value subscriber you'll save money several ways. First, all regular monthly selections will be billed at the low subscriber price of just $2.75 each. That's at least a savings of $4.50 each month below the publishers price. Second, there is never any shipping, handling or other hidden charges—*Free home delivery*. What's more there is no minimum number of books you must buy, you may return any selection for full credit and you can cancel your subscription at any time. A TRUE VALUE!

A special offer for people who enjoy reading the best Westerns published today.

WESTERNS!

NO OBLIGATION

Mail the coupon below

To start your subscription and receive 2 FREE WESTERNS, fill out the coupon below and mail it today. We'll send your first shipment which includes 2 FREE BOOKS as soon as we receive it.

Mail To: **True Value Home Subscription Services, Inc.** P.O. Box 5235
120 Brighton Road, Clifton, New Jersey 07015-5235

YES! I want to start reviewing the very best Westerns being published today. Send me my first shipment of 6 Westerns for me to preview FREE for 10 days. If I decide to keep them, I'll pay for just 4 of the books at the low subscriber price of $2.75 each; a total $11.00 (a $21.00 value). Then each month I'll receive the 6 newest and best Westerns to preview Free for 10 days. If I'm not satisfied I may return them within 10 days and owe nothing. Otherwise I'll be billed at the special low subscriber rate of $2.75 each; a total of $16.50 (at least a $21.00 value) and save $4.50 off the publisher's price. There are never any shipping, handling or other hidden charges. I understand I am under no obligation to purchase any number of books and I can cancel my subscription at any time, no questions asked. In any case the 2 FREE books are mine to keep.

Name _____

Street Address _____ Apt. No. _____

City _____ State _____ Zip Code _____

Telephone _____

Signature _____
(if under 18 parent or guardian must sign)

Terms and prices subject to change. Orders subject
to acceptance by True Value Home Subscription
Services, Inc.

11702-1